Three to Get Ready

Skye Warren

Prologue

Geneva, many years ago

THE KNOCK CAME a few minutes before six, a furtive rap of knuckles.

Her sister would be first to the bottom of the stairs. She was always first.

Geneva was second, but always on time.

No one wanted to face dinner with her father when he was angry. But she had reached a very good part of her book, and so she kept reading a few more paragraphs. Another sentence. A final word. Each one dropped like a gem into her open palms.

This was her way out of the house. She didn't sneak out at night like Caroline or even dream about going to college. She existed in the pages of a book.

She had another few minutes to spare, at least

thirty seconds, when the roar of an engine at the front of the house caught her attention. She dropped the book and ran to the window to see her brother step out of an Aston Martin and toss his keys in his hand.

Oh no. Every muscle in her body warned her not to go downstairs.

Nothing good would happen.

She had no choice. A quick glance at the clock showed the minute hand pointing almost to the top, the second tick, tick, ticking away around the full circle.

A quick glance in the mirror showed that her hair had come undone from the plait she'd used earlier. Her father would definitely notice.

Or maybe he wouldn't now that Geoffrey was home.

She sprinted downstairs following the curve of cold marble steps rather than the rasp of all of a sudden carpet and landed in her spot next to her sister. They both stood waiting outside the dining room where they could not enter until they had passed inspection.

Already the sound of male voices arguing could be heard from Papa's study.

Apparently, Geoffrey had wasted no time in finding their father.

She couldn't make out the words, only the angry timbre. Her father's commanding. Her brother's arguing. It was enough to make the wood panels shiver around her.

She glanced at Caroline, who was staring resolutely ahead.

"Why did he come back?" her sister whispered.

"The same reason he always comes back," Geneva said. "Because he ran out of money."

Papa liked them to be very still, even though it was hard. Her leg wanted to jiggle. Her gaze wanted to wander. She wasn't supposed to do that though.

She was supposed to stand like a statue.

Papa swept into the hallway, his heels hitting the marble hard, fists swinging at his sides. He usually frowned, but he wore an even deeper scowl. Geneva forced her face not to show anything. No fear. That would only make it worse.

Benedict James Roosevelt III liked fear a little too much.

She knew that was wrong, the same way she knew that gravity existed. Nothing she did was going to change it. The only thing she could do was learn how to use it.

Her father always started with Caroline. She was two years older, but she didn't think that was really why. He started with her sister because she was perfect. There wasn't a strand of blonde hair out of place in her braid. Her shoes were extra shiny.

Even so, he gave her a severe look. "What's your name?"

"Caroline May Roosevelt, sir."

"And what does that mean? Your grandmother's name, on my side. A cousin, on the other side. Your last name. Well, that's just something you borrowed from me, isn't it?"

Sometimes Papa did this. He asked questions that you aren't supposed to answer. I never knew for sure when it's happening, but Caroline always did.

She looked straight ahead without speaking.

It was the right answer. Father's eyes glowed with approval. "You're a sum of your parts, girl. Which means you have intelligence. Strength. Beauty."

"Yes, sir."

She didn't say thank you, because he wasn't complimenting her. Not really.

He was complimenting himself.

His gray eyes narrowed at Geneva, as if he

could hear her thoughts. She quickly looked ahead again, at the tiny crack in the paint she often used to mark the time. It was interesting, that crack. Interesting that a fault could exist in her father's perfect life.

It made her wonder what would happen if someone were to put pressure on the crack.

Would it break?

"There are two parents," he said. "Not one. Which means you have other qualities. Worse qualities. Such as? Would you care to tell me what they are, Caroline?"

Her sister said nothing, even though it felt like this was a question that needed an answer.

"I can," Geneva said, to cover up the silence.

Papa stepped in front of her, eyebrow raised. "Tell me."

"We're weak," she said, as if reciting a poem. "And romantic. And soft."

He stared at her for a long moment. He might backhand her. It felt like that kind of moment. Then suddenly he smiled. Or what passed for a smile on this man. A slight, almost cruel curve of his thin lips. "That's right, Geneva."

She flushed under the approval, even though she shouldn't care.

Sometimes she hated her father, but she always loved him.

She said the words that had been drilled into her. "We must push aside our baser natures in order to fulfill our role in the world."

His mouth formed a hard line again. "That's right. Which includes keeping your hair neat and tidy." He reached up to tug—hard—on her hair. She winced. His hand remained at her temple. He brushed his thumb over her forehead.

It was the most he'd touched her in years.

"You are growing up," he murmured under his breath.

A chill ran down her back. She forced herself to stay very still.

He pulled back. Not to hit her. He did the almost-smile again. "You can sit at my right hand today, Geneva. A special for you."

Geneva ducked her head as they went into the dining room. The place of honor normally went to Caroline. She met her sister's eyes briefly. She didn't recognize the expression that Caroline had. It wasn't jealousy or anger. It was concern, she realized.

Her heart thudded against her chest. She looked down, half expecting to see the heavy beat against the fabric of her dress. But there was nothing. No outward signs as she sat across from her brother, their father at the head of the table.

Caroline sat on her brother's other side, diagonal.

It would have been better if that's all there was. If there were only four people sitting at the long table. But there, on the end, always sat the memory of her mother. She was almost a real presence. They never even looked in that direction, as if she might see.

She didn't agree with her father about a lot of things, but she agreed to one thing: her mother was weak. If Geneva had a family, if she had children, she would never abandon them. Not even for love. That was for sure.

Geoffrey scarfed down the filet mignon, which was made rare, the way her father preferred. Her sister had cooked the steaks. Geneva had been in charge of the mashed potatoes.

She nudged the pink slab on her plate.

"So," her brother said, eyeing her. "Do they have a nanny or something?"

"They attend school. Surely you remember it, from before you dropped out."

An eye roll. "I mean when they're not at school. Who takes care of them?"

"They take care of themselves," her father said, his voice tight. "They are not silly little children who need to be coddled. They are young women who understand their place in the world, who understand their responsibilities."

Her brother snorted. "Isn't Geneva eight years old?"

"I'm ten," I said, offended.

"Your sister Caroline has breasts now. Or haven't you noticed?"

Geoffrey made a face. "No, I haven't fucking noticed."

"Watch your mouth, young man. It's nothing to be ashamed of, as long as a woman knows her place. Her breasts are for feeding her children."

"This family is so fucked up," Geoffrey said.

Her father slammed his fist on the table, making Geneva jump. She kept her gaze on the plate of red meat, ignoring the churning in her stomach. She envied her sister in her far-away seat. This close, she could feel his rage like waves in an ocean.

"This family," her father said, "is not a right. It's a privilege. One that you enjoy when you're over in California with your whores and your drugs."

"It's called a startup, Dad."

"It's a sinkhole, judging from the money I'm pouring into it."

"Personal computing is going to be the future."

Her father waved a hand. "A bunch of foolishness. Made by a bunch of fools."

Geoffrey looked away, his jaw clenching.

"Stand up," her father said, gesturing at her.

Geneva pushed back her chair and stood, hiding her tremble. "Yes, sir?"

"State your purpose, loud enough so your brother can hear."

"My purpose is to marry well and have children."

Geoffrey didn't even look at her. He didn't look at her father, either. "Christ. You have them trained like little wind-up dolls. It isn't right, you being in this big house with just the two of them. They need a—"

"A what? A mother? They have a mother, for all the good she did them. Do you see her out there in California? Do you see her fucking her boyfriend?"

"Yeah, Dad." Geoffrey's voice is brittle. "We see each other all the time and laugh about what a loser you are for getting left behind."

Her father's hand shot out. He slapped her brother across the face. Geoffrey continued facing down as red bloomed on his cheek. He was breathing hard. That was his only movement.

"Don't think you can disrespect me, boy. I don't care how old you get. You will obey me under this roof." He takes a bite of steak. "Now, do you want to talk about your sisters? Or do you want to beg me for the next check?"

Her brother was silent in the long seconds that followed, his answer clear.

He wanted the check.

Papa gave a satisfied grunt. "Girls, you're dismissed."

I wasted no time carrying my plate to the kitchen, but even so my sister reached the stairs first. When we got upstairs, I passed my room and followed her into hers. I shut the door behind us, holding my breath until the knob turned all the way.

Caroline tossed herself on the bed, letting her head fall over the side. She looked different upside down. "I can't wait until we get out of here."

With her body flat on the bed, I could see that my father was right.

My sister had gotten breasts.

"I can't wait until we get out of here," I say.

She turned right side up, leaning her elbows on the comforter. "So we can get married and have babies," she says on an eye roll. "Because that's all we're good for."

Her sister had other plans. Bigger plans. She wanted to go to college, but Papa wouldn't make that easy. She had some ideas about that, but I'm not like her. I'm just trying to survive long enough to get out of here.

I plopped beside her on the bed. "I want to have my own house. And a family, too."

"No way. I don't want more of this."

"It doesn't have to be like that," I said. "It doesn't have to be like our parent's marriage. You'll see. If you fall in love, it doesn't have to hurt. Love makes everything better."

Chapter One

Eva

I'M AT THE eye of the hurricane. It's strangely peaceful, watching everyone swirl around me. Peaceful as long as I don't acknowledge the wreckage the storm makes of my life.

It's not my family who's making a mess, though.

Not this time.

They're trying to help, but there's no fixing this.

"We bombard them with lawsuits," my brother Leo's saying. "So many they can't make a single move, can't write a single word, can't publish a single photo."

"I don't know," Sophia says, looking at her phone. "Eva looks pretty good in these photos. She's giving young Elizabeth Taylor hounded by the press outside a glamorous old world movie premiere vibes."

"Thanks," I say, my tone dry.

It doesn't seem to register in the conversation.

That's the way it's been since this little family meeting started.

"Leverage," Lucian says. "We apply leverage in the right places. Extreme force on very specific pressure points. That's how we get this to stop. Otherwise why have I spent most of my life acquiring sensitive information on powerful people?"

"I thought it was like a hobby," Sophia says.

Lucian gives her a smirk.

"As much as I appreciate a little well-placed leverage," my father Bryant Morelli says, "there are too many players to keep this quiet. The barn doors are already open."

"Which is why I think we should all go home and have a good night's sleep," I say, even though no one's listening to me. "The PR disaster will still be there in the morning."

"We have to act now," my mother says, proving that at least someone's hearing me, even if she isn't respecting my wishes. Her hands wring together in the very picture of maternal panic. "Before it gets any more out of hand. Before this turns into an international scandal."

"The Hughes family is worth a couple hundred billion dollars, Mother." Leo doesn't pull any punches. But then he never does. "It's already an international scandal."

There's something almost nostalgic about this war room. I presided over my fair share of them, but usually it was my parents or my siblings who were the subject of scandal. I can reminisce on the times when I was the one standing, the one pacing, the one making decisions. Now I'm seated on the couch while Leo paces. He's the default next leader now that I'm the cause of the drama. Or more specifically, my fiancé is the cause.

I touch the diamond on my fourth finger, turning the ring around and around. It's a heavy piece. A family heirloom. A symbol of the way he's bound to the Hughes family secrets.

And the way I'm now bound to them as well.

"I don't know why we don't just stick with no comment," I say. "We can sort through a thousand possible statements, but that always ends up being the best."

"Listen," Lucian says. "Elaine has barred me from murdering anyone these days, but I feel sure she'd make an exception for this situation. I'll call her."

Bryant snorts. "A Constantine."

Lucian's dark eyes flash. "She's a Morelli now."

My father's eyebrows rise in silent challenge. It's an old argument, though. One without teeth considering there's now a grandchild with Constantine blood. And my father, for all his terrible actions, is a pretty decent grandfather. He swaddles his granddaughter in a muslin blanket decorated with stars and moons. And now he'll have another grandchild.

I press a hand to my stomach, where I still can't feel anything.

No bump. No telltale kicks.

There's the morning sickness, though. Plenty of that.

"We do need to worry about the Constantines," my mother says, her voice soft. It quiets the rest of the family. "One in particular. Finn's mother, Geneva, is a Hughes now, but she was a Constantine before that. And you know that after a decades-long stretch of travel she's back at home. She's at the Hughes estate right now, advising Finn."

Sophia shifts, looking uncomfortable. "That did occur to me."

"What occurred to you?" I ask.

The room grows quiet.

I look around the room at my family. Many of my siblings have married, but the room is empty of them for various reasons. Mostly related to their children and the fact that it's almost midnight. Bryant and Sarah Morelli have eight children. Lucian, Leo, Sophia, and I are present. Lisbetta is listening from outside the door, banished because she's the youngest. I'm not sure where Tiernan is, and based on some of his past activities, I'm not sure I want to know.

Carter is overseas, like he usually is. And for some, he's been out of communication. That's been worrying Leo, though he doesn't like to show concern for our brother.

It's my father who breaks the taut silence. "They're referring to the possibility that Hughes disavows responsibility for the child."

I sit up straighter. "Excuse me?"

Sophia gives an apologetic grimace. "If there really is a Hughes curse, the fact that there's a child would only add fodder for the tabloids."

"There is no Hughes curse," I say.

No one meets my eyes. Not even Leo, the traitor.

"I'm serious. It's science, not some mystical malediction."

Sarah Morelli sighs. "You know I've always liked Phineas. I'm the one who urged you to go out with him that night at the gala. Now I regret it. Look what it's brought down on us."

"It's not your fault, Mom."

The door opens. Tiernan sweeps in, wearing a suit and looking as forbidding as usual with his scar and his scowl. "I've discovered the leak," he says without preamble. "A server at the sandwich shop Eva frequents for lunch suspected based on her switch from deli meat to a vegetarian. She speculated to a friend, who works for an online magazine called GossipGuy."

Lucian shakes his head. "We were felled by deli meat. It's a sad day for the Morellis."

"The friend, who attends NYU as a Communications major, tailed Eva to the Women's Hospital where she had her prenatal appointment. When he saw Finn enter, he suspected they were there for a pregnancy. He later verified it with a nurse who works for the doctor's office."

"Thank you," Bryant says, his voice grave.

Tiernan nods. I suppose I should have guessed that he was out gathering information at the behest of our father. That was his role for years, my father's own live-in muscle, with a loyalty that surpassed even blood. The loyalty of a bastard trying to prove himself. Since then he's broken away, become his own man, but old habits die hard.

"Surprisingly thorough journalism for GossipGuy," Sophia says. "I'm impressed."

Lucian gives her a dark look. "We'll get the nurse fired, obviously. Their license revoked. I know I'm in the minority with physical threats, but a civil suit at least."

"I'll handle the journalist," Leo says with a dark smile.

"Absolutely not." I stand up. "There will be no retribution for this."

"Eva," Leo says, protest plain in his eyes.

"I'm serious. This has gone far enough. Our response? It's no comment. We could hire the most expensive public relations expert in the world, and we have done that, in the past. The same people who advised the Kennedys. And guess what the answer is? A hundred thousand dollars later, it boils down to no comment."

"We should at least get her fired," Leo says, looking frustrated.

I stand up, ready to end this evening. "It's sweet that you all gathered for me, that you want to protect me, but I don't need protecting. I'm fine." I put a hand to my stomach. "And my baby is fine, free from any fake family curse. That's the most important thing. Right?"

"Of course," my mother says, but there's still worry in her green eyes. Her red hair and fair skin reflect her Irish heritage. She's the only one who doesn't have the Morelli black hair and dark eyes in the room.

"What good would it do to take vengeance on some poor deli worker?"

"Vengeance is its own reward." This from Lucian.

"Well, I refuse. And I insist that none of you do it either." I take a deep breath. "And as for Finn, I'm one hundred percent sure that he's going to claim the baby. He has his faults, but he takes care of his responsibilities."

I sweep from the room following that statement, startling Lizzy who stumbles backward, her cheeks red from getting caught. "Eva," she gasps. "I'm sorry."

"Don't worry about it," I murmur. "But you should go to bed."

Leo follows me into the hallway, closing the front on the hum of conversation in the drawing room. "Scram," he tells our youngest sister, not without affection. He waits until she rolls her eyes and heads upstairs before speaking again. "Are you so sure of Hughes?"

"Yes."

"Have you spoken to him?"

"I texted him."

His expression darkens. "And he ghosted you?"

"He didn't ghost me. It's only been a few hours since the news broke. He's probably busy. You know, salvaging the stock and reputation of a massive global corporation. Protecting his brother and parents from the press. You know, small little errands."

"You should be the most important thing in his life."

"He has a lot of responsibilities. And like I said, he takes them very seriously."

"I would let everything burn for Haley."

That makes me smile. "But here you are, at one a.m., at your parents' mansion, to help your sister in this hellfire broth she's found herself in."

"That's different. She's safe at home with our child. And our security team."

"Finn knows I can take care of myself."

"That's not the point. You shouldn't have to."

"Let's argue gender norms another day, brother mine." The truth is it has made me uncomfortable that Finn hasn't texted me back.

Not because I want him to sweep me away like some caveman, but because I'm worried about him. This secret has been the scaffolding of his life for so long. He was trained for it. Almost brainwashed into it. What is he feeling now that it's been destroyed? "Besides, where's Daphne? I'm surprised she hasn't texted."

Leo looks away, seeming guilty. "I haven't told her."

"Oh. But you called everyone else here."

He sighs. "She's married to Emerson. And Emerson's brother Will works for Hughes."

Outrage makes my throat tight. "So what? She's a Morelli. She would never do or say anything to harm me, Leo. You should know better than that."

"Stand down," he says, his voice dry. "It's not that I questioned her loyalty. I knew she would do anything for this family. I also knew she was invited to a cookout on the beach with her husband's brother tonight. She mentioned it in a text when she invited Haley to join them. I didn't want her to feel like she had to choose."

"She would have chosen us," I say, challenge in my voice.

"I know," he says with a sigh. "But for just one more night she didn't have to."

"Daphne's a grown woman."

"I know that." A longer sigh. "Maybe I'm still coming to terms with it."

It will probably be a lifelong struggle. It's not ordinary sibling protectiveness that guides him. Leo and I stood in for our parents when they were trapped in their cycle of drama and abuse. We raised our younger siblings, and it's hard to let go of that mantle.

"Everything is going to be okay," I say.

My brother smiles, a little sad. "You were always the one who kept us together. The one who fixed everything. It kills me that I can't fix this for you."

"Nothing is broken," I say, though it feels like a lie on my tongue. "Finn and I are stronger than ever. This won't change anything."

He shakes his head. "I wish I could believe you."

I wish that, too. "Trust me."

"Finn better do right by you, or else I will lift Elaine's murder ban."

"You'll do no such thing." I flutter my fingers, feeling the gentle bite of the gold and diamonds on the ring. It loops around my finger, propelled by my thumb. "But more importantly, it won't be necessary. Finn Hughes will come out on top."

I know how Leo thinks, how he works.

For him, love is a massive, violent act. It's burning the world down.

With me and Finn, it's quieter. It's different, even if I wish it might be louder.

I get into the black Suburban with a member of close security. The professional driver takes me back into the city, to my loft in Tribeca. And the entire time, my phone is silent.

No calls from Finn.

No texts.

Nothing.

Chapter Two

Finn

Why does it say retirement on the sign? I'm not retiring. I'm not old enough for that. I have work to do. I wasn't finished. Where is my secretary? Where is my office?

The CEO suite at the top of the Hughes Tower is designed to impress, at least for a visitor. Only once you spend more time there would you know about the back rooms—the lounge area, the restroom with shower, the bedroom to grab a few hours of sleep when pulling an all-nighter. There's even a small workout room with weights and a Peloton for the CEO to break a sweat without his subordinates looking on.

What is the reason for the elaborate, luxurious suite?

Convenience, certainly. A busy CEO of a

multi-billion-dollar conglomerate doesn't have time for a commute. Or even a trip down the elevators to the company gym on the 11th floor.

There's another reason. It's not a good look for the CEO to be huffing and puffing alongside his workers. It might be democratic, but a corporation isn't a democracy.

It's a dictatorship. A benevolent one, sure. But a dictatorship, nonetheless.

That's never been clearer than right now, as we discuss the fate of the company—its divisions, its subsidiaries, its hundreds of thousands of employees—from the top floor.

My father sits behind his desk, sorting through papers that my secretary found from somewhere. The discard bin next to the copy machine, possibly.

He studies a graph, his brow furrowed. He's still wearing his suit from earlier today. From his retirement party. Well, he's fully retired now.

No chance of coming back from that.

What's going on here? Is this some kind of episode?

I just dealt with this with my Dad. Alzheimer's. Or dementia.

How long has he been like this? How long, Finn?

My secretary was already aware of the situation. She's one of less than thirty people—lawyers, doctors, nurses, and family members who know about the situation. She patiently hands him sheets, some of which he reads, others he signs and hands back.

"Thank you, Ilsa," I say quietly.

She gives me a gentle smile. "It's all right, Mr. Hughes. People are confused right now, but you've always shepherded us well. Everyone will remember that."

I wish I had her faith. Or maybe I don't.

As awful as this disaster is, there's a terrible relief as well.

That I don't have to hide any longer.

The hum of conversation rises to a fever pitch, and I turn away from my father.

I should be with Eva.

That certainty sits in my bones. I should be with her, helping her through this, or at least sitting with her in silence if I can't make it better. Holding space for this. For her, and also for me. She's where I belong, my true north. Except that I can't.

I'm supposed to be this other person, this crisis-managing CEO.

Seated at a small conference table are five people, all people who knew about the situation before today. The company's head of counsel, Heidi Moreland, holds court. She's relatively young for her position, at forty-five but ambitious and highly competent. I promoted her a few years ago. Our family lawyer, Douglas Karl, is an older man with white hair and a neatly trimmed white beard. He was hired by my father, which means his primary job was to wait for an information leak.

"We always knew this would happen," Karl says. "Eventually."

"There are protections in place." This from Moreland. "I've already spoken with the FTC, but we have a bigger problem. A much bigger problem than legal."

"The court of public opinion," says Caitlyn Laurie.

She's one of life's great ironies. A more brusque and occasionally outright rude person you'll never meet, but somehow she excels at her job as the Chief Communications Officer. She knows what the public is thinking before they do. And she has a fantastic sense of how to deal with them in order to get the goodwill and support we want.

Which means that if she's worried, we're in big trouble.

I should be fully focused on this, but my heart beats a different song. *Eva, Eva, Eva.* I force myself to put my phone in my pocket, silent after the flood of notifications—stockholders, press, and reporters all clamoring for a quote, and force myself to focus.

I'm used to denying myself what I really want, anyway.

Laurie continues, "If we had controlled the flow of information, we might have had a chance in hell. Now anything we say is going to look like damage control. Which it is."

She knows as well as I do why we never came out with a statement. In fact she even supported the idea, knowing the backlash would be inevitable.

"What do you recommend now?" I ask, my voice even.

She sighs. "We claim that he had sporadic episodes. Rare episodes. Emphasis on rare. And that he made arrangements to step down as soon as he knew, et cetera, et cetera. That you've been beside him at the helm."

"That won't be enough to allay fears." That's Moreland.

Karl shakes his head. "He's still younger than most senators. If they're going to doubt him, they would have to doubt everyone in charge."

"It's easier when they have a face to blame."

Everyone looks at me, because I'm the face to blame. Somehow, despite only doing what my father demanded, despite holding the corporation together for over a decade, despite higher profits and bonuses than ever, this is my fault.

Laurie studies me, her shrewd eyes narrowed. "Naturally the last few major deals will be recast with this information. That new development in Tokyo. The launch of the home automation brand. The acquisition of that venture capital fund."

"Summit," I say. "The owner, Will Leblanc, has some trouble with corporate life. He's used to being in charge and hasn't figured out how to make a difference here. Yet. It's common to have an adjustment period. I'm sure he'd come around, but it could be a problem."

"You think he's going to challenge the acquisition?" Moreland asks.

"I would be surprised if he didn't call his lawyer before he left the building."

He was at the retirement party. He had a front-row seat to the drama.

He's also the brother-in-law of Eva, though I'm not supposed to be thinking about her. She's what I really want, my greatest desire, which is proof that I can't have her. Didn't I learn that lesson from my father? Didn't he show me how it would end?

I'm late for my meeting. I don't know who the hell you people are. My son is supposed to be here. Phineas. Where the hell is he? What did you people do with him?

"Fuck," Laurie says.

"But we're covered," Karl argues. "Any agreement Phineas brokered and signed is binding. He's had Power of Attorney since he was a teenager."

"That's precisely the kind of conspiracy theory bullshit that we don't want to have to tell the public," Laurie says, her voice grim.

Moreland shifts, uncomfortable. "We'd win in a court of law, but I agree with Laurie. If it gets that far, we're already screwed. Discovery alone would be a bloodbath."

Laurie snorts. "And a deposition? Where opposing counsel is allowed to ask any questions that are even remotely relevant? We're going to get fucked without lube."

"I would say Leblanc has enough grounds to bring it to trial."

"Which means that even if the verdict goes in

our favor, we're fucked." Laurie raises her eyebrows in cool challenge. "Do you think you can keep Leblanc in line?"

Maybe. I could probably handle someone like him—half temper, half ambition.

I thought he could be a huge asset to Hughes Financial Services. I still think so, but first he would have to figure out how to work within this new system. He'd gone from being a lone cowboy to working in a massive ranch.

A learning curve was natural. Assuming he wanted to learn.

This situation is infinitely more complicated, though.

Because he's family. Sort of.

His brother is married to Daphne Morelli, the younger sister of Eva. Which means any conflict between us can get personal, real fast. What if Will puts pressure on his brother to make the deal go away? What if this situation puts strain between Eva and her sister?

Eva's going to be punished enough, being with a man like me.

"What if we don't argue with Leblanc?" I offer, as casual as if I'm playing devil's advocate. "What if we give him back Summit the same way we found them?"

"And validate every doubt in the public's mind about this company's leadership? Absolutely fucking not. We keep them at all costs."

There's murmuring of agreement around the table.

I push away from the table and stand at the floor-to-ceiling windows, where dusk has already settled over the city. This is a real dumpster fire, but like Karl said, we always knew it would come to this. Secrets have a way of coming out.

Even if it wasn't happening now, they would know eventually. Once the curse took me. Once the curse takes Hemingway. Without heirs the company would pass out of our family's hands. And eventually someone would whisper.

Whispers become shouts.

Press has been camped outside the Hughes Tower for hours. I imagine they'll be there for days, for weeks. Even months. The story is worth it. Even a snapshot of me looking harried. Or worse, a photo of my father. I glance back where he's now coloring on a graph of the Hughes stock values. From this angle the drawing looks like an elephant.

A whisper of anger moves through me.

The truth is that I'm pissed. I'm pissed that my father made all these decisions, back when I was still a child. I'm pissed that he extracted these promises that I'm honor-bound to keep, when I was too young to fully understand the implications.

The anger is pointless, of course. It's pointless toward a man who's currently drawing a pink elephant and a blue palm tree and a green sun with dry erase markers.

My phone vibrates. I look down and open the messages on my phone.

Are you okay?

Eva has sent me a handful of texts since the news broke, mostly asking if I'm okay and if there's anything she can do. She's a better woman than I deserve, but somehow she's mine.

Unless she leaves you, the same way your mother left your father.

I wouldn't blame her, though. It would be easier if she did. The life of a caregiver is thankless, the embodiment of constant grief. Then again, what I know with my mind is different from what I yearn for with my heart.

And what I yearn for is... a future.

A future with Eva and the unborn child she carries.

No, I'm not okay. But I don't want to tell her and make her worry. And I promised myself that I wouldn't lie to her. That's the one thing she's owed as my fiancée. The truth.

"At least they're only looking as far as Daniel." Laurie speaks to the group, but I can hear her from here. "If we can portray Phineas as a strong enough leader, we can look forward to a short, intense firestorm followed by relative peace. And he has the reputation and good business sense to make people confident in his abilities."

"No one will know about the curse." This from Karl, who sounds hopeful. "And now that Phineas has a child coming, we'll be able to seamlessly hand it to the next generation."

Seamless. That's one word for it, the sleepless nights, the weight of the world on my shoulders when I should have been more focused on making out with a cheerleader.

Of course, I do have an heir. The beautiful Eva Morelli carries him around inside her. He'll no doubt be afflicted by the same curse, despite what she thinks and hopes. But no matter what I won't raise him the way I was raised. "He'll be free to choose his profession," I say to the room without turning. It's a promise to them as well as to me. And Eva. "Free to choose his life. Free to choose his secrets, without worrying about keeping mine."

There's a knock on the door.

The temperature of the room noticeably cools. Everyone here was read into the situation. Whoever's coming now? Probably wasn't, which means they're experiencing the same shock and anger that everyone is.

Moreland calls for the person to enter.

Alex Wong enters. He's been my CIO, the newest member of the C-Suite. And the most hotheaded. Just what this party needs. He surveys the room with an accusatory look. "I see who should be named on the lawsuit. All of you are complicit."

The accusation makes the room feel electric.

"This is a private meeting," Moreland says, her voice businesslike.

Wong snorts. "I'm here in my official capacity as Chief Information Officer. Trust me, I've considered resigning. I've written the draft on my phone, but... for reasons beyond my comprehension, I'm still here. Which means I have to do my fiduciary duty."

Laurie gives him a dark look. "Which is?"

"To make sure you've seen what's on the news."

Moreland waves her hand. "What do you think we've been discussing?"

"Not about Hughes." Wong meets my gaze, looking angry but also conflicted. "Not about Daniel Hughes, the former CEO of Hughes Industries. This is about Phineas."

There's a collective silent shock. Fuck.

"What about me?" I manage to ask, sounding unconcerned.

Wong takes a deep breath. "They're saying that Daniel's condition is hereditary. That you have it, too. That your grandfather did, too. Something called the Hughes curse."

Chapter Three

Finn

There's a particular quiet at four in the morning.

Even the nightclub scene sleeps now.

Everyone has made their way into their beds—or into someone else's bed.

An eerie dark hangs above the skyscrapers. A few intrepid reporters are camped behind the Hughes building. They rush out of their folding chairs and vans, cameras flashing in my rearview mirror.

And then nothing.

It's too late for most people. Too early for just about everyone.

Somewhere, surely, bakers make bread. Housekeepers fold sheets. Nurses and doctors tend to the sick. But they are absent from the streets. I pass miles of black windows. The streets are slick with rain I don't remember falling. Or maybe that's just dew. The same drops that would have dotted blades of grass, had there been any greenery in sight. Instead it coats concrete and glass. It makes the road glitter in my headlights.

I don't really have a plan when I leave Hughes Industries.

Generally speaking I should probably go home. Dad is asleep. His nurse has been sending me text updates since I brought him home this afternoon. I'd hated leaving him, but the office was in an uproar. They needed leadership.

Unfortunately, they were stuck with me.

I didn't want to be there any more than they wanted me there, but we all had to play our parts. That's the irony of a birthright. It's a gift. One you can't turn down.

No doubt my mother has waited up for me.

Hemingway, too.

I should go home to reassure them… of what? That the fallout wouldn't be a huge fucking deal? I can't do that. It would be a lie, because it is a big deal.

And you know what? It should be.

We lied.

Why shouldn't we take responsibility for that?

Why shouldn't we apologize?

That's what we teach children, as young as kindergarten and preschool. If you lie, say you're sorry. If you make a mistake, apologize.

Then we grow up, and every word has to be parsed by the legal department.

Not to mention Public Relations.

Every move we make is about image. The bullshit about shareholders and employers is just a modern-day version of noblesse oblige.

The reality is simpler.

We covered up the Hughes curse to hide our own shame.

To cower from our own mortality.

Well, here it is. I'm driving through the streets of New York City in a Bugatti. No lawyers. No C-level executives. Not even family with me now.

If I were to die now, I'd die alone.

My hands turn the steering wheel. I glide forward and brake at all the right spots, but it doesn't take me out to Bishop's Landing. Instead I end up in Tribeca, in the garage of an old building. The doorman gives me a curt nod. There's no flash of recognition. No glee that he'll have a story to tell or satisfaction at seeing someone powerful brought low. Which probably just means he didn't have a chance to watch the news before he hit the night shift.

I use the key that Eva gave me to let myself in, feeling like a thief. A criminal. A fucking imposter. That's what I am, pretending to be a man who deserves a woman like her.

Moonlight through the tall windows makes exaggerated shadows from her elaborate décor. Her aunt's décor. Most people would accept a two-million-dollar loft as inheritance. And most people would have redecorated by now. I don't even think it's her taste, but she keeps it this way. She preserves her aunt's legacy.

Birthright. It comes in many forms: money or property or secrets.

And we're stuck with it, whether we like it or not.

The pungent scent of soil emanates from a corner table. A terrarium in a blown glass jar is in the middle of assembly, with little piles of gravel spread out beside a bowl of moss. A pastel-colored gnome waits patiently for placement.

Eva can't help taking care of everything and everyone.

It's her strength.

And her weakness.

Even her hobbies are about creating sanctuary.

I leave my briefcase, my wallet, and my keys

beside the gnome.

Her bedroom is in the back, away from the windows. Bric-a-brac covered walls form a room, but they don't reach the ceiling of the loft. Inside the bedroom, there are no decorations. No polka dot giraffes and retro neon signs. Only a bed with white sheets.

A wild spill of black hair is a sharp contrast against the silk.

It makes my chest squeeze.

I undress down to my briefs and climb into bed, pulling her warm body close. She shifts, drowsy, murmuring something. "Shh," I say, my voice low. "Keep sleeping."

For a moment, it works.

She rests in my arms, sleepy and still. I breathe her in. But it can't last. Nothing ever does. She stretches, her body lithe against mine. Her warm womanly scent makes my cock hard, but it's more than that. It makes my chest feel full. What kind of emotion is that? Love?

She gives a slow, drowsy blink. "Finn?"

"I'm sorry."

"Don't... be." She turns in my embrace, her movements languid. "Are you okay? I called you, but you didn't answer."

"I'm a bastard." She must have been afraid

when the reporters cornered her outside her work. Anyone would have been. The fact that she's plenty strong enough to face down the fucking paparazzi doesn't mean it's acceptable.

I want to rage at them for even speaking to her, for upsetting her.

I want to rage at her, but somehow we're in this polite, cultured conversation.

She sits up. Her face is completely in shadow. I can only guess at her expression. I can only imagine her beautiful eyes and gorgeous smile. Shadows draw her hair and the curve of her waist. "Phineas Galileo Hughes. I was so worried about you. How dare you keep me waiting? I almost showed up at your office."

"You and half the employees at Hughes Industries. There would have been a line."

"It wouldn't have stopped me."

A faint smile touches my lips. It probably wouldn't have stopped her. And I would have paid a lot of money to see Eva Morelli take on Alex Wong and Caitlyn Laurie. It would almost be worth it, but I can't let her fight my battles.

Bad enough that she's been injured because of them.

My smile fades. "I'm sorry. I could leave. Say the word, and I'll go."

Her arms tighten around me. "Don't."

"Then at least we can talk about this." Even though for me, there's nothing to discuss. Our ending was written in the stars a long time ago. But I'll give her this, because it's the only thing I can. She can rail at me. "This isn't what you signed up for."

She pulls back. Her eyes are dark pools of liquid, deeper than the earth itself. "This is exactly what I signed up for. The hard times along with the good times. What do you think marriage is?"

"We aren't married yet."

"A technicality."

"An important one when it comes to spousal privilege."

She grows still. "It won't come to a court trial."

"There are people already calling the attorney general and FTC. They want one."

"They can keep waiting," she says, as fierce as a lioness. "You didn't do anything illegal. Or anything unethical, for that matter. You have a right to your privacy. So does your father, especially when it comes to his medical condition. How am I the only one who's heard of HIPPA?"

I would have loved to see her face off against Heidi Moreland. "The outcome of the case doesn't matter. Or whether there even is a case. As soon as people see the Hughes family as tainted, shares will fall. They already have."

"Yes," she says, her voice dry. "Your net worth fell a few billion dollars today. But don't worry, darling. I have enough money to keep you in suits and Bugattis."

I smile in the darkness. The Hughes fortune may have lost a few billion, but we have several more billion in less liquid assets. Which means I can afford my own Bugattis, but I still wouldn't mind being kept by this woman. "Should I have dinner on the table when you get home? Maybe I can learn to bake."

"I do love a devil's food cake."

"I know."

She gives a feminine snort. "How?"

"It was served as the Morelli Christmas Gala cake a few years ago."

"Two years ago," she says, sounding confused. "Why would you even remember that?"

"Normally you don't eat much at the galas. You're always busy working the room, smiling and laughing and talking to people. Making them feel at home, which is quite a feat in the gilded ballroom in the mansion. If you even take a slice of cake off a tray, it's to hand it to someone's great aunt. But that night you had not one but two slices."

She pulls all the way back, almost sitting up. "How would you know that?"

"Because I was there. I noticed you. I always noticed you."

Incredulous. "Why?"

Now I'm the one incredulous. I lift myself on my elbow. "What the hell do you mean—why? Because you're fucking gorgeous. And I'm a man."

"But you never acted like you were interested in me."

I fall back on the bed, staring up at the ceiling. "Because it could never go anywhere."

She brings my hand to her stomach, which is still almost flat. I rub my thumb over lace, enthralled by the warmth of her. The miracle of her. "Turns out you were wrong."

"Turns out I was wrong," I agree softly, wrapping my hand around her waist and pulling her until she's straddling me. The ends of her long hair tickle my chest. I reach behind her neck and tug. Then her lips are on mine. I should surrender this moment, but even now, underneath her, I take over. I claim her with my lips, my tongue, my teeth.

I was wrong when I thought I couldn't have you.

I was wrong when I thought I could ever give you up.

Lying to the press. Keeping my family secrets. Running Hughes Industries. I did those things for my father. And for his own form of responsibility, which involved pretending for the sake of the stock market. None of that was for me, but this? Now?

This kiss is entirely selfish. I touch my lips to hers because I can. Because I want her. Because she tastes like memory, and I never want to forget.

"Finn," she says, pulling back to look at me. "Are you okay? Really?"

I touch two fingers to the side of her neck. And then lower, my palm running between her breasts. Down to her stomach, which feels almost as flat as it ever was.

Barely even a bump, but somewhere inside her is a child. Our child.

"Of course I am."

"Finn," she says, exasperated, annoyed. Good. She should see what a bastard she has in me. She should leave me, the way my own mother told her.

"Rough day at the office," I say, my tone saying *business as usual.*

"I care about you."

"You care about me," I ask, gently mocking. "Because you're a good little wife. Dutiful. Pliant." As if to underscore that fact I reach between her legs. No panties. She's warm. Wet. I was teasing her, perhaps, but it's the truth. "I want to take it out on you, and you don't mind. Do you?"

She melts beneath my touch, spreading her legs so I can reach her better. What did I do to deserve her? That's simple. Nothing. Eva isn't the kind of woman a man could earn. She's a gift.

"Shh," she says. "It's okay. I'm here. I'm yours."

That's when I realize I'm making sounds. Rough sounds. Groans as I rut against her, pushing my cock against her thigh. Grunts, like a fucking caveman. Tearing into her nightgown like an animal. And what's worse, I can't stop. I used to be a polished, inquisitive lover. All that's gone. The veneer, stripped away.

All that's left is pure, stark need.

Chapter Four

Finn

I SHOULD CONTINUE the politeness the way it started, all solicitousness and quiet concern. I should do that but something in me is fracturing. I'm not even gentle as I flip her over so that she's hugging the plush mattress.

Her plump ass rises in a sight that's both erotic and profound.

Usually I like her facing me. I like her touching me.

But the way I'm feeling right now, I want her to lie submissive while I mount her. I push her legs further apart with my knees. My hands are on her hips, holding her steady.

She grips the sheet, her knuckles white from how tight she's holding on.

From this angle I can only see a heavy fall of

dark hair and the barest hint of her profile.

Part of me misses the eye contact, but maybe I need her turned away—for how roughly I'm going to use her. Maybe I can't let her see me like this, losing control.

My cock notches against her sex.

I should make sure she's more ready. With my hands. With my mouth. Normally I'd do that, but right now I can't wait. I slide home. Her inner muscles clench around my cock. She gasps as her entire body stiffens.

In apology I reach beneath her and find her clit.

"Finn."

It's almost enough. Almost enough to hold myself inside her, without thrusting, without fucking. Letting the sweet pulses of her climax caress me. Orgasm runs through her like an electric current. She collapses against the bed, trapping my hand. So I keep toying with that pearl. She jerks in protest. Too sensitive. Well, too fucking bad.

"Sorry," I say, though there's no remorse in my voice. No remorse anywhere in my body. It would be physically impossible to wish for anything but this, her pussy warm and welcoming and tight. "This is what you signed up for, remember? To have me." I push against her, making her gasp. "To hold." A pinch of her clit has her clenching around me, a velvet fist.

"Please," she says, begging.

It's not entirely clear whether she's begging me to make her come again. Or whether she's begging me to stop. I'm afraid to ask for clarification, because I'm not sure I could stop. The basest part of me has taken over. Mine, it says.

I bite down where her neck meets her shoulder. She bucks beneath me, but it doesn't dislodge my cock. I'm too deep inside her now. I never want to leave.

"Please," she gasps out. "Please. More."

I drop my forehead to her back. "You're a goddamn miracle."

She pushes her ass back, tempting me. "It hurts."

It hurts. In my chest, mostly. In my cock, too. I reach down farther to where my body joins hers. I force two fingers inside her pussy, even as my cock remains lodged inside her. It's an incredibly tight fit, my cock and two fingers. Enough that she pants as I stretch her sensitive skin, but even then she doesn't push me away. It strikes me that she would let me do anything to her. I could tie her up. I could share her. I could make her my sexual plaything, but here's the irony. My deepest fantasy is to make her my wife.

The heel of my palm pushes on her clit. My fingertips brush against a sensitive place inside her. She comes in a hard shudder and keening sound. I hold her tight through the waves, gritting my teeth against the need to come.

Then she collapses again.

I pull out, my cock still hard and glistening with desire.

Fuck, it's hard to leave that warmth.

The only way I can do it is because I know I'll come back. All night. That's how long I plan to use this woman. That's how long I'm going to make her do her wifely duty, even though we aren't really married yet. I turn her over, revealing glorious breasts made glistening with exertion. Her legs are splayed in satiated abandon. If only I was done with her. If only.

"Finn," she says, breathless and tragic.

We should talk about what happened.

As if I'd waste time on empty words and broken promises, when we could have this.

I take my cock into my fist, stroking slow and long, reminding myself that I have a long time. Not forever. God, not that. But I have hours tonight. And maybe tomorrow. How many tomorrows after that? It doesn't do any good to dwell. "Here," I say, touching her flushed and swollen pussy. "That's what I want to do next. Taste you. Make you moan. Feel you come on my tongue. I especially want the part where you squirm away because it's too much, but I don't let you."

Her cheeks flush. "But I already came."

That makes me laugh, though it sounds faintly despairing. "This isn't for you, sweetheart. I thought you'd figure that out. This is for me, tasting you, hearing you beg. And then? Hmm. If I make you come again… and again… and again… you'll beg for me to stop, won't you? You'll need a moment to breathe, so I think I'll use that time to fuck those pretty breasts."

Her eyes are wide. I'm not usually so crude. Experimental, sure. Playful. But always with care and respect and a measure of restraint. There's nothing holding me back now.

I pinch her nipple between my thumb and forefinger. "You'll let me do that, won't you? You'll let me straddle you and push my big, throbbing cock between your breasts, you'll let me press them together so you can take me to heaven, won't you?"

She looks at me with those gorgeous doe eyes,

flustered and turned on. "Yes. Maybe."

My smile feels cruel. "Let's find out how you feel about it."

I push between her legs and find her wet. It's incriminating, that pool of want. She's so slick for the idea of my cock between her breasts. There's something demeaning about using her that way, but there's something powerless, too. As if I can't even hold myself back from rutting against her. Like her breasts are my sexual lodestone.

"Eva Honorata Morelli," I say, half taunting, half reverent. "I think you love this."

I press my face against her sex, breathing her in. Woman. Spice.

A long lick from the bottom to the top. She squirms right off the bed.

God, this is fun. Not in the charming way of illegal gambling dens or underground fights. Those are thrills. This is a bone-deep satisfaction. I worry at her clit with my tongue. She bucks away from me, but I've already planned for that. I have my forearm over her, keeping her pinned, holding her steady for my licks.

I make her come once and then twice.

I make her come a third time, while she fills the room with her cries.

And then I'm climbing over her, straddling

her. Pushing my cock between her breasts. Tweaking her nipples so her eyes glaze over. It only takes one stroke, two, and then I'm coming in long white ropes across her perfectly pale skin, a slash of cum across her plump red lips.

CHAPTER FIVE

Eva

I WAKE UP full of contentment.

There are a million reasons to be worried right now, from the PR disaster to the financial ramifications with Hughes Industries. But I can't be too upset with the abrasions from Finn's scruff still stinging my breasts.

I'm warmed by him, both inside and out. Sated. Replete.

There's a new coolness. That's what wakes me.

Finn's body had wrapped around me for a deep slumber, but now there's only the cool silkiness of the sheets. What the hell? With my eyes still closed, I reach out my hand. Groping fingers touch the still-warm bed. I peek one eye open.

Finn sits at the edge, revealing the hard line of his back.

It's a relaxed position, the kind someone might use to ponder their day, but nothing about him is relaxed. Every muscle looks taut. The air crackles with tension. It was more than the temperature that woke me. It was him.

He'd been different last night, more raw. More himself, I think.

Our sex has always felt incredible, but it was also… considerate. Playful sex. Feminist sex. What happened last night was filthy. I lost count of the number of times he woke me up and all the ways he used me. I'm sore in secret places.

"Hey," I say, my voice a little hoarse.

He looks back, hazel eyes dark. "Go back to sleep."

I glance at the clock. Five o'clock in the morning. "Come with me."

A suggestion of a smile. "Can't."

"Duty calls?"

"Something like that."

"You should let my family help. They've weathered scandal."

"Not like this."

No, not like this. Our companies are privately held, for one thing. We don't have shareholders to answer to. The Morellis also have a reputation for scandal, so it's easy enough to handle one more. The Hughes family is seen as above reproach. They're more than economic leaders. They're seen as moral leaders, which makes the fall that much further.

Part of me wants to soothe him however I can, but I also know better than to offer false platitudes. People are freaking out, and it's only going to get worse. Everyone will want a piece of him. The media. His enemies. Even his friends.

He runs a hand through his hair. "I failed him."

"Your father?"

"This was what he asked of me. What I promised him. That I would keep the world from knowing his secret, and now… And now there's no way to bottle it back up."

My heart thuds at the thought of a little boy tasked with such a big promise. Like Atlas, carrying the weight of the world on his shoulders. His legacy was both a gift and a millstone. "Maybe… maybe it's a good thing. Maybe you can set down the promise now."

His shoulders twitch as if he's testing the weight on them. "And it doesn't matter because he won't know the difference? But I know the difference."

It would matter to an honorable man. That's Finn. "People can make mistakes."

A snort.

"I don't mean you. I mean him. He shouldn't have asked that of you."

Finn shook his head, not allowing me to absolve him of guilt. "There's going to be hell to pay the next few months. And he's not going to bear the brunt of it. You are."

I sit up in bed, pulling the lace-edged sheets to cover my breasts. "I'm fine."

His gaze dips low. Desire flushes his cheeks. "You're strong enough to take whatever I give you, aren't you?" he asks, his voice gone thick.

"Is that what last night was? Some kind of test?"

Erotic memories hover in the air between us, a sensual specter. It makes me blush even as he holds my direct gaze. "No, sweetheart. I'm done acting like I can walk away from this."

My heart squeezes in both pleasure and pain.

He may be staying with me, but part of him still resists it. He gives more credence to the Hughes curse than I do, but at least he's here. I suppose that's all I can have for now. And for as long as we have. I'll show him that it can last forever. I'll prove the curse wrong, day by day.

"Come back to bed," I say.

His gaze darkens. "I'd love to, but we have a big meeting at six."

I groan. "I have a busy day at the fund, too. Oh, remember to bring your tux for the Morelli Fund Gala. It's black tie, naturally."

He leans across the bed and kisses me. It starts off small and questing. It turns long. And marauding, his lips moving over my cheek and down my neck until I'm breathing hard. He pulls back and looks me in the eye. "People will talk, if we're seen together."

They would do more than talk.

The press will shout questions as we go inside. Most people will be nice, but some may take surreptitious photos and videos while we're eating. An anonymous waitress or busboy will end up giving a quote to TMZ, speculating that we were worried or fighting.

"Let them talk," I say, lifting my chin.

"Fuck," he mutters, kissing me again.

"What?" I ask, panting against his lips.

"I really do have to go, or I would show you what I think of that beautiful defiance."

My body pulses with reminders, pleasantly tired muscles ready to be used again. "Go to your meeting, then. Show them who's boss, Phineas Galileo Hughes."

"The gala is about celebrating you," he says. "I don't want to distract from that."

"Listen. We tried it your way. Or more specifically, your father's way. It didn't work. Now let's try it the Morelli way. Brazen it out. Show them we don't care."

There's uncertainty, but he nods. "Fine, then. A tux. The gala."

"Really?" I can't hide my surprise.

He turns back. "You didn't think I'd come?"

"I didn't think you'd let me help. You're always so self-contained, so sure that you can handle anything. Even when you told me about the curse, it was only information. You didn't really let me in. But I can help. I want to."

A pause. Then a nod. "Okay, we brazen it out."

I flop back onto the mattress while he stands up. There's one more hour of sleep in my future before I have to get dressed. But first I get to enjoy the show of Finn's bare, muscular backside. He's lean and hard packed, full of muscle and tightly-leashed energy.

Control matters more to him than brute strength.

He stretches in the orange-tinged dawn, unselfconscious.

A few steps across hardwood floors.

Then he opens a connecting door, steps out of the room, and closes it behind him.

I stare at the door, stunned. A myriad of emotions run through me, each more alarming than the last. Surprise. Fear. Grief. This isn't the first time he's slept over at my loft. There's a routine. When he gets up from bed the first place he goes is the bathroom. Or maybe, at a stretch, if he forgot his briefcase, which contains his change of clothes, in the living room, around the tall dividing wall.

Instead he stepped into my closet.

There's nothing but a jumble of clothes in there, ballgowns and pantsuits and workout clothes. No room at all for even a spare drawer for Finn's clothes. Which means there's no reason for him to step inside. He didn't do it hesitantly, either. Not like someone exploring or hunting for something in a new place. He walked in decisively, as if it was the bathroom. As if he was one hundred percent sure it was the bathroom.

It's a mistake anyone could make.

It doesn't mean anything. It certainly doesn't mean that the Hughes curse is striking, that the disease is happening and happening now. It doesn't mean that I'm losing him.

There's a beat of ringing awareness.

Then the door opens, more slowly this time.

Finn steps out, his expression severe. And resigned.

It scares me more than the mistake, that resignation. If he believes it, then it's as good as true. "Finn," I say, my voice unsteady. "Let's talk about this."

"There's nothing to talk about."

"Yes, there is. It doesn't mean anything."

"All right," he says, too readily.

"I'm serious. You've been here… what? A couple dozen times? It's not like you need to have the floor plan memorized. Not to mention it's five a.m. Not exactly a time known for the best focus. Plus you have a lot on your mind right now."

His lips curve without humor. "Who are you trying to convince, Eva?"

I subside, not sure of the answer. "Oh God," I whisper.

He crosses the room and gives me a kiss, this one so different from the others. He doesn't kiss me on the lips or brush his mouth along my neck. Instead he kisses my forehead. It's acceptance, that kiss. Acceptance of something that I can't even name.

But he has no such hesitation.

"If it's now, then it's now," he says, his tone gentle. "If it's later, then it's later. I'm not going to count. And I'm sure as hell not going to get worked up every time I make a misstep."

"No?" I ask, because I feel pretty worked up myself.

"I'd rather enjoy my time, Eva. With you."

You're mine now, for as long as we have.

The truth is, I hadn't really believed in the Hughes curse. It sounded like an urban legend. How could the line always produce boys? Surely some little Hughes girl had once been born, even if it wasn't on the right side of the sheets. And how could every single one have the disease? Genetics were about chances, not about guarantees. We couldn't know for sure that Finn would get early-onset dementia. We couldn't know that the unborn child inside my stomach, the one currently the size of a tennis ball, would get it. That glimmer of hope had been enough for me. I could have built a life on that glimmer. And I had.

But now it felt more real.

It felt like a third person in the room, living and breathing. Directing the course of our lives.

Taking him from me even as he stood in the room, naked and powerful.

"This is okay," I say, throwing the sheet off. Heading into the closet. Ignoring the fact that it's on a different wall entirely than the bathroom door. Pretending not to notice that it's painted with pink and white polka dots, with a glossy pink lion door knocker on it. It looks nothing like the leather-wrapped door to the bathroom. My great aunt had not put a lot of stock in subtlety. I threw open the door and grabbed a power suit from the rack.

"Eva." His voice held a gentle warning.

It's possible I was freaking out. "This is fine. Because you know what I do? I solve problems for my family. I do it all the time. I've done it as long as I can remember. And I'm going to solve this, because you're my family now."

I press my palms to my stomach. I'm as naked as Finn, and suddenly I know why some ancient warriors fought naked. I'm stronger like this than with any fabric or metal armor. Terrified and terrifying at the same time.

A mother bear whose cub has just been threatened.

"Don't get your hopes up," he says softly. "If this could be solved by money, we'd have done it by now. Millions spent on research. Billions. It hasn't helped."

"How is that possible?" I ask, half angry, half despairing.

"Some problems can't be solved."

I could see that he believed it. Forbearance was written into the lines of his strong, handsome body. He made a glorious sacrifice on the altar of responsible capitalism, but I refused to let him go. And I had no such belief about the limitations of my problem-solving abilities. I had kept my parents from murdering each other a thousand times over. I'd saved my siblings from jail and violence and public condemnation. I had put the Morelli name on hospitals and public parks and libraries, using our power to move mountains.

I would solve this problem, too.

One pernicious disease.

One family curse.

One heartbeat to the next, praying it's long enough.

Chapter Six

Finn

I'M WEARING MY best suit. It's priceless, quite literally.

It was made by a famous designer who mostly serves as a figurehead now, with legions of designer underlings who actually create each season in his style.

"*Bellissimo,*" he said when I visited his Mediterranean villa. "*Il tuo forma è bellissimo.*"

"*Grazie.*"

He appraised me in a thorough and mostly asexual way, his eyes cataloging every measurement. I couldn't pass up the opportunity for a bespoke suit. I went on a few dates with his daughter, in between business meetings. The real estate investor I was courting for the Hughes expansion into China was American-born, but she spent most of her time on the island of Crete. Stunning blue ocean and pebbled beaches.

It had been a complicated existence, half playboy, half CEO.

It was a role built to satisfy the curiosity of spectators. I was responsible enough to run the business, but I got into the tabloids enough to prove that I was getting mentorship from my father. After all, he wouldn't hand over the reins without oversight. Not Daniel Hughes, devoted company man. I played the role of capitalist heir to the hilt.

And then the mask was ripped away.

I fought it, but I can't help but be relieved that it's happened.

It was inevitable, really. The only surprising thing is that it took this long.

I'm in my office, waiting. Waiting. Waiting for the right moment to face an angry mob. In this case an angry mob of other suit-wearing men and women. They're gathering downstairs, right below me. The C-level executives and senior VPs are filing into leather swivel chairs around a gleaming cherry-wood table.

It won't be like before, in my office. That had been tense, but everyone there wanted a resolution. The people downstairs? Some of them want blood. That's what feels fair. And I would give it to them, if it was only me at stake. But it's more. It's always been about more. My father. My mother. Hemingway. The rest of the Hughes.

Every employee in the building and around the world.

And now Eva. Our child. It's about them now, too.

I'm standing at the floor-to-ceiling windows, looking out over Manhattan.

All I want to do is be with Eva. Have I lost my drive? My will to run this company?

Did I only ever do it for my father?

As if she senses my indecision, my phone vibrates. It's Eva.

"You holding up?" she asks.

Not really. "It's just another day at the office."

"Bullshit," she says softly, the coarse word sounding elegant in her voice.

"They're going to skin me alive," I say, rueful. "No one would look forward to it, but it needs to be done in order to move forward."

"What are you going to say to them?"

"Honestly? I'm thinking they're owed an apology."

"An apology? Now *that's* bullshit."

A reluctant smile curves my lips. "If only you

were in the room."

"I will be," she says. "In spirit. Pretend I'm there, giving them hell. You gave more bonuses and commissions than your father ever did. People got rich under your leadership, and you know what else? They enjoyed their jobs. Don't apologize for that."

I sigh. "The money doesn't seem to matter."

"Money always matters."

"Spoken like a Morelli," I say, gently teasing.

"No," she says. "Spoken like a soon-to-be Hughes."

"Well, the Hugheses aren't big on second chances."

"I like second chances, but that's not what this is. Where was the first chance? You never got to be a regular CEO. You were always doing what everyone else wanted. Your father. The board. The employees. And now they're mad about it. What would you do if it wasn't about the curse? What would you do if you were just leading the company?"

"It's too much of a stretch," I admit quietly. "It's never been about that."

"Listen," she says, her voice serious. "I know things seem bad now, but they're going to get better. Once they're over the surprise, and the fear, they're going to remember how great of a leader you've been. They're going to remember who's been signing their paychecks. And most of all, they're going to remember who's been steady as a rock."

I knew they were angry, but I didn't think about the fear.

But it's real. It's brutal. I had so much fear for my father, even knowing that I was losing him. I was never able to really accept it, even as it happened. It didn't occur to me that it's what the stockholders and executives are facing, too. They're having to confront my father's mortality. The nature of human frailty. We aren't immortal. We're infinitely breakable. And here is a man who had such money and such power. If even he could be broken, what hope does anyone have?

Fear explains some of the anger, but it won't make it easier to face.

"Love you," I murmur.

"Love you," she says, then her voice turns hard. "Now, go give them hell."

I head downstairs, knowing that they're all assembled.

Alex Wong stands at the head of the table. He goes quiet as I step inside, which probably means he was stirring up trouble. We have a brief staredown, which ends with him taking a seat along the wall. It's a win, albeit a small one.

Eva was right.

This meeting isn't about apologies or second chances.

It's about leadership.

"Thank you for coming," I say. "This is a tough time in Hughes Industries history, and I'm here to listen to you. To answer you. To do my best to ease your concerns."

I recognize every face in this room. I know they're names, their GPAs from college, their retirement portfolios. I've played ball with their children and sat in quiet vigil during illness. Maybe they won't remember those parts. Or maybe they won't matter enough, but they matter to me. That's worth something, those memories. Knowing that I could help, if only in small ways.

"But what I'm not going to be is your punching bag."

This makes people exchange glances.

"You want one of those, head to the boxing ring. I'm not going to apologize to you for my father's illness. Or even for keeping it a secret. Everything we did was legal, and more importantly in my view, we believed it was right. That decision paid for your yacht," I say to the head of marketing. "And for your daughter to go to Duke," I say to another. "And for your son to get a prosthetic when he came home from active duty."

There's a murmur through the room. Some agreement, some people saying that I bring up good points. Others say it's distracting from the real issues.

"So ask your questions," I say. "Tell me your concerns. Let's face them together. I'm here for that and for those hard conversations. I'm here as long as it takes."

There's a stool, and I prop myself on it. I'm serious about staying as long as it takes. I can't offer them an apology, but I can give them my undivided attention. A hand goes up at the back of the room. Jordan Beaty. A good man. A little timid. Which means the question will be a soft one. "Will you remain the CEO of Hughes Industries?"

"Absolutely," I say. "Next question."

Annalise Jacobs negotiates leases valued in the millions. "Do you want to remain the CEO of Hughes Industries?"

That makes me crack a smile. Trust her to get to the heart of the issues. "I was born for this position. Trained for it. Everything in my life led to this moment, so who would I be without it? I've wondered about it. I would be lying if I said I hadn't."

"We're all wondering about it." A mutter from Wong.

I ignore it. "My father taught me that the life of a leader is one of service. I don't sit in the office upstairs because I need more money." There's a few nervous laughs around the room, acknowledging that I'm one of the wealthiest men in the world. "I do it because my father instilled in me the values of Hughes Industries. Loyalty. Responsibility."

"What about your responsibilities to your employees?"

I turn to Wong. "What about them?"

"You abandoned us."

With only a slightly exaggerated motion I look around. "I'm here, aren't I?"

His expression turns dark. "This is only an empty gesture. It isn't real."

A soft laugh escapes me. "What's real, then? The words we send over email? The digital signatures we put on contracts? Those things aren't more real than this. Fifty people in a room, all of us worried. It takes on a life of its own, fear. We think we can fight it, but it's like fighting air.

Because you're right about one thing. The words don't matter. Actions do."

Wong scoffs.

Will Leblanc has been sitting in the back of the room. Eva's brother-in-law. Which means that when we marry, he'll be family, too.

He stands up. "We can't trust anything you say."

"Bullshit."

The word rings across the massive conference space. I recognize the voice, even though I can't credit it. I can't believe that my father is here. How is he dressed in a triple-breasted suit with antique gold buttons and tasseled loafers? Except for thinning hair and slight shadows under his eyes, he looks almost the same as when he last stood in this room.

His eyes are completely clear.

He spares me only a brief glance before coming to stand beside me. "Bullshit," he repeats, more softly this time. He doesn't need to speak loud, though. They're all leaning forward to catch his every word. He has charisma, this man. Natural leadership. "You can't trust him? When he was seven years old he broke a priceless vase at a friend's house. He could have kept it a secret, but he came into the room calmly, set down the largest piece, and swore he would cut their grass until the vase was paid for. As far as I know he still goes there every two weeks with his Weedwacker. It was Ming Dynasty."

There are a few laughs. He's funny. Somehow, I'd almost forgotten that about my father. I'd lived with the childlike stand-in for so long that it's strange to see him act normal.

Hemingway came in behind him.

I dip my head and speak low. "What the hell is going on?"

My brother shrugs. "He woke up like this. And he insisted on coming once he found out what you were doing. I figured it might help."

It might help, or it might blow up in our faces. Either way, I'm glad. Glad to see my father like this, even if it only lasts for a few hours. Or a few minutes.

It's as much a reunion for me as it is for the others in the room, even though I saw my father at dinner last night. Or I saw the version of him that he is mostly now.

My father stares down everyone in the room. Even Wong squirms in his chair. "I gave this company, I gave you the best years of my life. A whole hell of a lot of them. And I gave you my son, a smart, competent leader who actually managed to raise our profit margin. Something I wouldn't have thought possible, because they weren't too shabby under me either. Is that what you object to? Do you want to give back the bonuses and stock options in a show of righteous indignation?"

Silence in the room. You can hear, albeit faintly, the whoosh of traffic below. Downstairs the streets are seething with exhaust air and busy people. Up here it's cool and silent.

"No," my father says, glancing at me. "I gave you Phineas Galileo Hughes, the best CEO that Hughes Industries has ever seen. He wants to hold this town hall so he can make you feel better about it, as if he's the one being disloyal here."

Phineas Galileo Hughes. You named him after a pirate and an astronomer, Eva once told him, even though he wasn't lucid at the time. Which means, I think, that you wanted him to have adventures. And to look up at the stars.

Some of the people are shamefaced.

Some are still angry, but they're holding their tongues.

I can't quite agree with my father's hard line. He comes from a different generation. But I appreciate the support. And it appears to be working. My dad steps outside, and Hemingway and I follow him. He looked smooth and confident inside, but now that he's here I can see a thin sweat break out across his forehead. "Get me home, Finn," he mutters.

"I'll take care of him," Hemingway says quickly. "The car is downstairs waiting."

I clap my father on the shoulder, my throat tight. He's already fading away in front of my eyes, the moment of lucidity fleeting. "Good to see you, Pops. I love you."

"You too," he says, his eyes already fogging up again.

I stare after him for too long a beat, emotion thick in my chest. I barely ever see my father these days, the real him. The good days come less and less often. And I sure as hell never expected to see him walk in here. Not before, at the faux retirement party, where he thought it was thirty years ago. No, this version of Daniel Hughes was every inch the leader.

This was his true retirement party.

He didn't need balloons and a cake. He needed to give his marching orders.

And I need to give mine.

Later I'll be able to sort through my emotions at seeing my father that way, at hearing him talk about me as his successor with such pride. Later

I'll be able to sit with both the pleasure and the ache of knowing it will never happen again. Grief.

For now, I turn to the assembled group. "You heard the man. Time to go to work."

Chapter Seven

Eva

The Morelli Fund has poured millions of dollars into the community—at-risk teens and literacy. Health care for women. We're focused on making a difference here in New York state, but we support endeavors all over the country. All over the world.

Each one comes with heartbreaking stories of people who weren't helped in time.

And inspirational stories of survival that bring tears to my eyes.

Each cause matters, but none has ever been more personal than this one.

We're seated in our conference room, but unlike regular conference rooms this one has plush chairs and a large TV that acts as our screen. There's soft yellow lighting and a series of paintings made by kids at the Children's Hospital framed on the wall.

When Leo first commissioned the building for us, he designed a regular conference table and chairs and fancy screen that slid down from the ceiling with a whir. But I realized quickly that some of the directors of charities, particularly the small ones, the ones most in need of funds, were intimidated by the room. They felt their pictures and documents weren't good enough because they weren't some super-slicked slide deck created by a grant consultant who was paid hundreds of dollars per hour. So I changed it up.

Draw something that you want to see when you get well and leave here.

That's what the nurse told the kids when they made these.

A horse galloping around a corral.

A litter of puppies chasing a ball.

A family at a picnic.

Hope. That's what they drew. The most innocent, pure form of hope.

That's what I need right now. Desperately.

Hope that I can find a solution for the problem I need fixed most—to know that Finn Hughes will live a long and happy life. And that my child will, too.

"We'll figure this out," Leo murmurs, sensing my tension.

He can always sense it. I make a noncommittal sound. There's no use pretending with him. Of course we will. I'm sure of it. I'm not worried. Those would be lies, and he would know.

"You've trained your whole life for this," he says, and I laugh.

That's true enough.

Saving people. Rescuing them. Whether it's a teen on the streets via the Morelli Fund or my father on a bender after seeing Caroline, I have made a lifetime out of helping solve things. But now would be the worst time to fail, and that steals my breath.

There's a knock and my assistant director, Stella, comes in, smiling as she leads in an older man with gray hair and a young woman who has the bearing of a doctor. I'm not sure what the bearing of a doctor is, precisely, a sort of godly confidence that doesn't appear overinflated. This is someone who deals in life and death every day, who doles it out.

The man turns out to be the manager of their facility, while the doctor is the head researcher on the team. They're partnered with Cornell but they're funded from multiple sources.

Including the Morelli Fund, if this meeting goes well.

There are other research organizations on dementia. Bigger ones. Ones with more equipped labs and more research papers credited to their scientists. I'll meet with them, too, but I have a gut feeling about this one.

I shake hands with them. So does Leo.

He doesn't usually sit in on my meetings. He's here for moral support.

Stella opens the meeting, providing a smooth introduction to the Morelli Fund with a little self-gratuitous celebration. "The Morelli family is responsible for helping thousands of people here in the city and beyond. They're a true treasure to the community."

Leo gives me a wry look, which I ignore.

"However," she says, "even with their resources, we have to make hard decisions. Whatever comes of this meeting, whether we can support you or whether we can't, we want you to succeed. Our decision isn't only based on the merit of your cause, or even your abilities, but also where we feel that we can provide the most value."

It's a let-down speech, designed to make them feel better, because we can't give to every cause.

And we won't. I'm not going to hedge our bets by putting a little bit of money into every single dementia organization. That would feel safer, but it would be worse.

No, I'm going to back the organization that has the most promise with the full might and fortune of the Morelli Fund. I'll pour my own money in if I have to. And the Hughes, who already donate a significant amount to the largest advocacy group.

I don't want platitudes.

I don't even want promises.

I want results.

They open with a relatively standard fare for these kinds of things. An estimated six million Americans are currently living with dementia, many who don't know about it. The signs and a person's natural reluctance to share the effects make it difficult to diagnose. And even harder to treat. The doctor is forthright and smart, which I like, but it's the man, the Manager of Operations for the research facility, who really surprises me.

"Alzheimer's is a broken record," he says, "playing the same song on repeat. It's a cacophony so loud and jarring that it makes you feel like you're going insane. It's a ticking clock, an incessant chime. It's an infinite number of sounds, all of them lonely."

"You sound like you're speaking from experience," I say.

He glances at the doctor, as if he's trying to keep his mouth shut.

I don't want that. "How do you know that?"

His name is Alistair. "My father suffered from it, and we tried every treatment. We went from doctor to doctor, all around the country, all around the world. We tried regular medicine and holistic treatments. Acupuncture. You name it."

Leo sits forward, putting his elbows on his knees. "And?"

"Some of it worked. Some of it didn't." He pauses. "Some of it made it worse."

The doctor gives him a severe look, as if in warning. "We have a strict regimen for studies, naturally," she says, turning to face me. "What he did with his father wasn't part of that. Let me tell you about a new treatment we've been testing."

"The one on injectable soluble amyloid beta proteins? I read that in the research journal where it was published. That's how I found you guys. I want to hear about his experiences."

After a long pause the doctor reluctantly nods. "It's not scientifically verified."

Leo gestures to the older man who's been

sitting there quietly, almost serenely. "This man's father seems to be living proof. Isn't that scientific?"

"Science isn't only about results," the doctor says. "There are a million anomalies and outliers. We're looking for repeatability. And a high success rate."

"One man doesn't count," I say softly, "except to that man. And his family."

The man gives me a faint smile. "Precisely."

"What did you find?" Leo asks, curious.

"There's a new treatment from a doctor in Sweden that shows promise, but he doesn't have the funding—not only funding. He doesn't have the certification or even the ability to manage studies of this magnitude. But the people he's treating with his approach toward inflammation of the brain are having incredible results. My father started having clearer days."

"Why isn't everyone talking about this?"

"Sometimes the side effects would be worse than the disease. Throwing up. Migraines so severe he couldn't stand up. Vertigo. Blood in the stool. Blacking out."

"Shit." This from Leo.

The doctor nods. "That's a major problem when it comes to testing."

"Tolerating the treatment," I say, having heard some of that before when it comes to acupuncture and herbs. That was before I even knew about these side effects.

"It's not easy," Alistair admits. "In fact it's hard as hell."

The doctor continues. "It takes over your life, some of these treatments. Which would be hard for most people to accept. And on top of that, we don't have enough studies to even prove that it works. Convincing people to even try is hard."

I lean forward. "What would it take to make those studies happen?"

"There's a number of roadblocks. Operational ones. Logistical ones. Scientific ones. It's not only the funding we'd need."

"Listen," I say, "I like science. I believe in it, obviously. That's why I'm here, talking to you. But I also believe in miracles. And magic coming from unexpected places. We aren't going to turn away from what might be the most important lead because it's hard."

The woman nods. "We research at the lab. We have a few test cases, but there's another problem we face when it comes to these sorts of tests. Time."

Time.

That's the one thing we don't have.

My baby may benefit from this, but Finn? God, he's so young and virile it's hard to imagine him being an invalid. I think of the way he walked right into the closet, so sure of it and so wrong. Was it a random mistake? People make them all the time. Or does it herald disaster? There's no way to know except to wait. There's no way to know except to watch more grains of sand fall to the bottom of the hourglass. We're running out of time.

I put a hand on my stomach, which has only the faintest bump.

This baby should know his father, not as an empty body.

As Finn, the man I love.

Alistair makes a wide gesture. "It's easy to say you'd do anything to get better, but I watched the results of that ravage my father's body. Even on the days his mind was clear, he struggled with the side effects, some of them short term, some of them long. The truth is, even finding people for studies can be hard, because some people don't want treatment."

"I understand that, and I'm not judging it. People have to do what works for their lives." One of the projects we fund is a hospice for those who choose not to pursue chemotherapy but are rejected by their families. Chemotherapy is fucking brutal, and depending on the stage of cancer, doesn't even have a high success rate. Sometimes it's harder for the families to give up even when it's the patient's choice for treatment. The irony isn't lost on me. "But surely some people want this treatment. Surely some would choose it, if it meant not getting dementia."

The doctor hesitates. "The truth is, I don't think it would be enough. To be clear, I think it will help. In fact that much has already been proven. But it only slows the progression."

A cure would be better, but it's not required.

Even more time… that would be enough.

"It sounds absolutely fucking insane, but that's not necessarily a bad thing. The sane methods haven't been working out particularly well. Is that what you pitched in the proposal?"

The doctor glances at Alistair with significance. They can feel the energy in the room building. "No," she says carefully. "We asked for a smaller study, something more manageable and with higher predictable odds of success. It does involve a distillation of the rehmannia root. We want to confirm the correlation between inflammation reduction and dementia severity."

That's important but too small to make a difference for Finn.

It's a stepping stone, and he needs the entire path.

"To test what she's talking about," Alistair says, "we would need to test in stages. We'd have to work with doctors here in the states as well as the FDA to prove that it's safe."

"Excuse me," I murmur, turning blindly to get up. I go to stand at the window, looking out over the landscape of New York City. Finn is out there, facing down angry stockholders. He's fighting that battle so I can fight this one.

Leo joins me at the window. "This feels big."

"It feels huge, but I don't know. The scope of the studies they're suggesting…"

"We can fund it."

"It might not be soon enough," I whisper.

He takes my hand and squeezes. "We'll get through this, sister mine. You'll make it happen. I have faith in you. Sometimes my faith in everything else, even God, has been shaken, but I've never lost faith in you. You saved me once. Now you'll save him."

Maybe I should accept Finn's illness. Maybe I should say goodbye. Part of him wants that from me, but I can't. And maybe it's not even a choice.

I'm acting from habit and fear.
And love.
Like everyone else.

Chapter Eight

Finn

The vaulted entrance hall has been festooned with orbs made of cracked gold and matte black. They're a startling contrast to the white marble that makes up the Waldorf Astoria ballroom. A chandelier with a thousand prisms hangs from the middle, reflecting a thousand points of light throughout the room.

The colorful fabric of the women's dresses reflect the shimmering light from the chandelier above. Men's suits are crisp and tailored, their ties matching their wives' sharp eyeliner. The ballroom is filled with a thousand people in expensive clothing, but none of them hold a candle to the woman on my arm.

Eva wears a flapper dress that shows off her incredible toned legs. I want them wrapped around me, but I have to put on a public face in front of all these people. They're staring at us, especially with all the press. So I can't steal her away into a dark corner and put my hands on the flowy fabric. It looks like silk or chiffon, with beadwork that accentuates her curves. It's the kind of dress that I want to leave on so that it reflects the light when I'm inside her, thrusting, working away at her, my cock snug in her warm cunt.

"Stop looking at me like that," she murmurs, a flush on her delicate cheekbones.

"Then stop looking so goddamn sexy."

We're still standing in the entrance, so I let my hand slip lower on her hip to brush her ass. This woman has a body that doesn't quit. It's hell taking her out in public, especially when the men look at her. Mine. I want to growl at them to avert their eyes, which is… strange. Amusing. Not entirely unpleasant. I've never felt jealousy before.

I feel like a caveman, which is ironic since I'm wearing a tuxedo and a hundred-thousand-dollar watch.

Eva leans toward me, her breasts warm against my arm. "Behave yourself," she whispers in my ear. Her voice is a pleasant purr that I feel like a stroke on my cock. "If you keep looking at me like that, my nipples are going to get hard, and then everyone will see through the fabric of this dress. I'm not wearing a bra."

I groan. "You're torturing me."

She laughs softly.

"I will behave," I say, my voice grim, "but only because this night is honoring you."

"It's honoring the Morelli Fund."

"You are the Morelli Fund."

She shakes her head, brushing off the praise. The Morellis get most of their positive press from the fund. The charitable family. The generous family. It wouldn't even exist if it weren't for her. And it sure as hell wouldn't give so much and be so effective. I'm proud as hell of what she's accomplished. What she continues to accomplish.

"I wouldn't even have come if not for that," I say. "They're all waiting for me to get confused and jump into the champagne fountain thinking it's a pool."

"Well, it probably would be refreshing," Eva says, going for a joke.

But I can see the worry in her luminous dark eyes. They're fringed by long, dark lashes. The dark irises seem to change colors, sometimes a deep chocolate. Other times, like now, a mysterious midnight. No matter the color, they always make me feel like I'm being drawn in. Like I'm drowning in a warm, pleasure-filled sea.

She's not really worried that I'm going to skinny dip in the champagne fountain, but she's remembering the morning when I walked into the closet. Was it a blip of dementia? Or was it simply a man exhausted and stressed out? There's no way to know, of course.

And it doesn't matter, in the end.

Whatever will happen will happen. I learned that early.

We move through the crowd, smiling at the right moments, laughing at the right times. I know how to work a crowd, and this crowd is ripe to be worked. All of them want a glimpse of the now-infamous Finn Hughes that they can pass on to their friends or whatever journalist they have on speed dial. It would be easy to be cynical, but Eva keeps me sane. She's a bright light of authentic caring in a sea of shallow, grasping ambition.

There's hunger in this room, despite the surface-level reason for the event. Charity. Giving. And yet I can smell the greed, the amount of money moving in the room. It's a heavy perfume scent, almost sickly in its sweetness. And familiar.

I grew up mired in this scent.

A hint of perfume, a hint of aftershave, a hint of alcohol.

The clink of wine glasses against crystal underlays the buzz of conversation.

All the Morellis are in attendance, including the patriarch Bryant and his wife Sarah. The former gives me a dark look. Like any man, he knows the thoughts I have for his daughter are filthy. And he wants better for her. We can agree on that much, but hell if I'll give her up.

"Evening," he says, reaching out a hand.

We shake.

Dimly I hear Eva's mother chatting to her about celebrities who showed up.

"Sir," I say, my voice low enough to be private even in a sea of people. This is the first time I've spoken with him since the news broke. "I imagine you have words for me."

Bryant gives me a narrow-eyed look. "I have more than words. Fists."

"While I think you're due to take a swing, for a couple of reasons, I'd ask you to wait until the evening is over, so we don't ruin it for Eva." And if he ever turned a fist on his daughter, I'll make sure it's the last thing he ever does. I still remember the time I walked in on them at a Christmas party, his hand tight around her wrist. It left a red mark.

He glances at her. "She's already had to deal with too much."

A string quartet in the corner strikes up a slow, drowsy song. "For what it's worth, I love her. And I'll do everything in my power to make this easier for her."

"Would you?"

"Yes."

He gives me a grim look. "People say they'll do anything for love, but once the costs start racking up, they're gone. It didn't work out, they say. We grew apart. That's what people say these days. They don't know about real love, lasting love."

It's strange to hear this man, this man with a renowned temper and disdain for all things emotional, talk about real love. Especially because his marriage is known to be a society match, arranged by their parents. Did they end up falling in love? They seem distant.

Maybe he's talking about someone else.

I'm not sure how to feel about Bryant Morelli and his cryptic comments. He was a cruel father, occasionally abusive, sometimes cruel, always manipulative. But Eva loves him. He'll be my child's grandfather. Can there be peace after so much violence? Is his concern for his daughter genuine? If it is, I owe it to him, and to her, to address it.

"I have a lot of flaws," I say, choosing my words with care. "I wouldn't wish myself on anyone, but one of my strengths is that I keep my promises. No matter what."

He grunts.

"And if you want proof of that, this entire scandal will work. My father extracted that promise from me when I was five years old—before I even really understood it. When I got older, when I was seven years old, ten years old. When I was sixteen years old I begged him to let me take it back, but he refused. A man keeps his promises, he said. And I agree."

"You weren't a man," he says. "You were a child."

"Close enough when you're a Hughes. We grow up fast."

"Because you don't have long," he says with a nod of brusque understanding. There's no sympathy in his gaze, which I appreciate. We aren't men to be pitied, either of us.

"When Eva and I get married, I'll take that promise just as seriously. There will never be another woman for me. And I'll let no other man touch her. Forever means forever."

For a moment he's silent, processing my sincerity. Then he snorts. "The Hugheses were always a bunch of pansies."

That makes me laugh, because it's the side of Bryant Morelli that I'm used to. Irreverent. Cold. But for just a moment I saw a glimpse of a deeper self he keeps hidden. I give Sarah Morelli outrageous comments and flirtation, which makes her smile and blush, before stealing Eva away.

The room is alive with conversations, the quiet hum of power players making deals over cocktails and clinking wine glasses. We stop and speak with her sister Sophia and wave to her brother Lucian. Her other siblings are here, too, but we don't see them.

We shake hands with some of the most powerful and influential people in the city. And in the world. Most of them already know me. And they already know Eva.

They praise her work, which just makes her demure. She speaks about the causes, skillfully praising and charming even the most tight-fisted of billionaires until they promise to fund a new hospital wing or a youth center.

Hours pass, and I wish I could leave.

The air is thick with the sounds of conversation. My feet sink into the plush carpet beneath. Sweat beads down my back. I can feel people's eyes on me, can almost hear their thoughts...

Is Finn Hughes losing his mind like his father did?

Is the family hiding more than a disease?

Can we trust them to hold up the economy?

Beneath the high vault of a glass dome we mingle until the hour grows late.

Around us people dance a waltz on a white stone-and-mosaic promenade.

White-aproned servers bring wine to people who sit and eat at the long tables. There are more of those cracked gold globes here. They flash in the dark light, as though beneath a brilliant and unsteady falling star.

A woman whose glasses look about an inch thick corners Eva, talking about a few millions dollars that she'd like to use to put her husband's name on something grand. Something everyone will still have to say for generations to come.

They're looking for immortality, these people.

And I can't blame them. I would be one of them, if there'd been even half a chance.

I'd take a lifetime with Eva if I could.

It didn't work out, they say. We grew apart.

There's a single pinpoint of light against the

backdrop of this disease, and that's that I know the value of time. A month. A day. A single second where I can look at Eva, give her a smile that's full of sensual knowledge, watch her get flustered as she talks to the older woman. This second? It's worth more than a thousand empty lifetimes.

With Eva still distracted, I'm introduced by an acquaintance to someone I haven't met before. A doctor. A brain surgeon, actually. Dr. Jenika Faulk. who seems nice enough, and an older gentleman next to her. They start talking to me, both seeming excited, about some project they're getting funded through the Morelli Fund. I give them an encouraging smile and ask a few polite questions, though I don't know the details.

"It was more than we dared to ask for," Dr. Faulk says.

"Eva is always generous," I say.

"It's more than generosity, I would say." This from the older gentleman named something that starts with an A. Aiden? Asher? He told me when we were introduced a few minutes ago, but now I can't remember exactly what it was.

Am I forgetting because of early-onset dementia?

Or because I've just met a few hundred people?

Most of my mind is already working on undressing Eva. I thought I'd keep the dress on her, but now I'm thinking it would be better off. I want her naked and wearing only the gold beaded high-heeled shoes she has on, the ones with the red bottoms. I want her on all fours, facing away from me, that beautiful curved ass high in the air.

"In this case, I hope you don't mind me saying, it's personal."

I stare at the man. "Alistair," I say suddenly, as the name comes to me.

"That's right," he says with a genial smile. "I bet you meet so many people at these things. I'm Alistair Thomas of the Tuffin Institute."

Suspicion builds in the back of my head. "The Tuffin Institute." I've heard something about it. From where? For what? "Isn't that for the study of brain diseases?"

"We focus on dementia. And once this study begins, it will change the game."

"I see."

The man is looking at me like a fellow prisoner, as if he knows exactly what I'm feeling. Except how can he? The woman is looking at me like I'm a specimen in a petri dish.

Fuck fuck fuck.

"If you'll excuse me…" I let the words trail off as I take my leave.

Blindly I take Eva's hand, dragging her away from the woman who's already monopolized too much of her time. I've been wanting to leave the gala, but I don't head toward the stairs. Instead I aim for the back. A quiet space. A dark room. A private moment between me and the woman who's made me her personal lost cause.

CHAPTER NINE

Eva

HE TAKES ME through the kitchens. Guests aren't allowed back here, but no one stops us. No one would stop Finn Hughes. Even if they don't recognize him, it's in his bearing. The way he walks, like a man who knows he belongs in any room.

The front of the hotel is glittering and gorgeous.

In the back it's bustling with activity. Concrete walls hold rows of silver appliances. He keeps going, my hand linked in his, past a row of offices with cardboard furniture and the colorful, cheap knickknacks that decorate them. Then we're back in the front of the hotel again, but on the other side, near ballrooms that aren't currently in use. It's quiet. Dark. The room is probably thirty thousand square feet. It's a place for wedding receptions and meetings. And right now, it's a place for us.

He faces me, his expression grim. "When were you going to tell me about Dr. Faulk?"

"You met her?"

"Dr. Faulk of the Tuffin Institute for Brain Health."

He doesn't seem mad, exactly.

He doesn't seem pleased, either.

Which isn't a surprise. The truth is that I wasn't planning on telling him, because he's not the only one who gets to keep secrets for the greater good. "We give money to lots of charities. I didn't know you wanted an itemized list."

He gives me a sardonic look. "And this was a random donation?"

"No," I murmur. "Nothing about it was random."

He turns away, staring at a blank concrete wall. "Damn it, Eva."

"You're mad because you think I'm interfering."

"No." He swings back to face me, his expression blistering in its intensity. "I'm worried because you're building up false hope, and you're going to be even more disappointed when it doesn't work."

Tears prick my eyes. "Why does hope have to be false?"

"Because we've been down this path. The Tuffin Institute was the recipient of our grants a few years back. They're one of the more... eccentric research facilities."

I lift my chin. "I think they're credible."

"Did they feed you some line about curing it?"

"No. They were... refreshingly honest. Even if some of what they said hurt. They said there's a promising new treatment, but it has serious side effects. Part of the study will be understanding how widespread those effects are, and if they can be managed."

"There's no cure for dementia, Eva."

"What about slowing it down?"

A low growl. "It will only make it harder if you won't accept the curse."

"And I think it will only make it harder if you do accept it."

He reaches up, and I can't help it. He's a large, strong man bristling with frustration. My history tells me what will happen, instinct kicking in before I can temper it with reason. I flinch, as if he's going to hit me. He freezes, his hand poised in the air where he was going to brush my cheek. An astonished expression is replaced by fury.

"I should have given him a beating," he growls, speaking of my father.

It's something of an open secret that Bryant Morelli, a man of belligerence and temper, has occasionally struck his children. He's gotten better about it. Mostly because Leo got old enough to fight back, and he protected all of us. He's also gotten a little calmer in his old age, but that doesn't erase the past. "What were you two talking about, anyway?"

"Ironically, I think he wanted assurance that I would treat you right."

Warmth wars with confusion. "He's a complicated man."

He shakes his head, his hazel eyes never leaving mine. "Men are simple. All of us. As long as you know what makes us tick."

"What makes you tick?" I whisper.

"You." He takes a step closer, crowding me while being careful to show me that I could escape him if I wanted to. He's commanding and obstinate, this man, but never violent.

He would never raise his hand to me.

Or our child.

I know that as truly as I know the sun will rise

tomorrow.

And yet... with the dementia, he might lash out. He might become violent and lash out, the way his father has before. It reminds me of the story of Jekyll and Hyde. Maybe every man has two sides to him, one hidden until it emerges unexpectedly.

"Me," I say, looking up at him.

In the shadows he looks impossibly handsome. "I don't want to hurt you more than I have to."

The statement resonates with truth. And with irony, because he will definitely hurt me. Maybe every husband will, though. There's no way to live a life, all the way to the very end, without experiencing some pain. Loss. Grief.

Saying goodbye will never be easy, not where love is involved.

"Have you heard of the Terminal Project?" I ask.

A pause. He nods.

"It's where the families won't accept a cancer patient's choice not to experience chemo and all the terrible side effects. It allows them a peaceful space to spend the rest of their time."

"Why are you telling me this?"

"Because I know the irony of what I'm doing

here. I support that project. The Morelli Fund does, anyway. And I believe in their mission, but there's something different here."

"Which is what?"

"The only reason you accept your illness is because you believe there's no alternative. You're not choosing between chemo and hospice. You're throwing up your hands."

"Where is the treatment, Eva? It doesn't exist. Hell, until a few years ago, they were damn sure dementia was caused by plaque in the brain. We poured all our money into studying that plaque, because the doctors were so damn sure."

Unfortunately I read about that. It feels a little like a conspiracy theory, except it's true. And tragic. A little secret keeping and a lot of desperation led the medical community to pursue that line of research for literally decades. Only recently did they reveal that some people with plaque don't have dementia. There's no correlation. Now they think it's a protein, but Finn isn't entirely wrong. It's still a guess. An unproven theory, which is why we need to support people who are developing new strategies.

"They have results that are incredible."

"A fluke. Or a lie." A humorless smile. "People lie sometimes."

THREE TO GET READY

He's accepted me and this baby with grace, but only because he's resigned to his fate. We're like his version of a hospice. We're the place he's going to rest before he loses himself.

He doesn't think he has a choice.

I'm determined to give him one. "Listen, I know your family works with a world-renowned doctor... but only one, right? You couldn't go knocking on the door of every dementia specialist in the country, because it would have risked the big secret."

"We donate huge amounts of money to research for a cure."

"That's not the same thing as asking for a personalized treatment plan."

He shakes his head. "It's not going to help."

"Why does it matter?" I ask. "So what if I'm wrong? So what if I pour money into the research and it doesn't pan out? We have enough money."

A rough sound. "You're going to say you're okay with this, but really you're not. You're going to dream of it being different. You're going to imagine and insist and eventually, eventually when you realize it won't happen, you'll resent me."

I shake my head, bewildered. "No, I won't."

"I watched it happen," he says, a little too

loud.

A hard swallow. "You mean your mother."

"She loved him. And she insisted the curse wasn't real. It was easy to pretend, because he never presented symptoms. Until he did. A forgotten name here. A stumble at a party there. She pretended it wasn't happening, at least until the major episodes started. Then she hated him."

"What do you want me to do? Lock you up in an asylum because you forgot where the bathroom was? Anyone could make that mistake."

"It would be better than denial."

I shake my head; this time I'm the one who doesn't break eye contact. "I'm not denying that it's happening. That's the opposite of what I'm doing. I'm recognizing there's a problem, and I'm going out to fix it. If you wanted a wife who waves sadly as you sail off into the sunset, then you picked the wrong woman. I'm too damn selfish for that."

He stares at me, breathing hard. Slowly, the hint of a smile breaks, like the reach of a single sunray through a storm. "Selfish, are you? Yes, that's how everyone describes Eva Honorata Morelli. She's always taking, never giving, never taking care of everyone."

"I'm not giving you up," I warn, trying to

sound stern.

"Is it because of the sex?" he asks, almost conversationally. His hands fit against my waist, pressing me flush against the cool wall. I lean back, almost desperate for that wash of relief. And then it's too cold. Too flat. Too hard when I prefer the scorching hot strength of him in front of me. Instead I lean forward—trapped, trapped, trapped. "Is it the orgasms I can give you? The way you melt on my tongue? Is it the way you gasp and cry and beg?"

I've lost my breath. I have only sensation. I pull it into my lungs, the pleasure and the pain. I let it nourish me, like a hard spring rain on fertile earth.

He leans close, close enough that I can only see shadowed angles. It becomes a feeling. Heat. Safety. And a piquant sense of danger. This large prowling male has been challenged, and he's going to make me regret it in the best possible way.

My hips push forward, almost on their own. His breath catches.

"I'm not the only one who gasps," I manage to say. I'm halfway lost. Almost entirely gone, but I have to challenge him back. He needs that, I think. I need it, too.

I don't decide to rub against him like a cat. It happens. It happens the same way I open my mouth and press it to his hard jaw. Even freshly shaven, I can feel the faint backward bristle on my sensitive lips. It raises every nerve ending through my body in quiescent waves.

His large hand cradles my breast. I can feel the tiny beads on the bodice as if they're imprints of his fingerprints. Like he's left his mark on me. My nipples feel tight and aching. None of my bras would work with this dress, but without it my breasts have been rubbed against silk all night like. Shifting, shifting. Making themselves ready for Finn to expose them and press starved, open kisses. A nip, and then I'm whimpering.

He laughs, an unholy sound in the dark. "Tell me again how selfish you are."

"I want—I want—" I can't finish the sentence. Maybe it's because I want too many things. Or maybe it's because he's found a rhythm, the heavy ridge of his erection against my clit. The feel of the beads on the fabric becomes a kind of sensual massage, sharpening the sensations to the point of pain.

"Tell me," he says, inherent threat in his voice.

Threat that he won't follow through. That

he'll stop.

I manage to find some words, a jumble of them. A pile. "More. Please. Yes."

"Good girl," he murmurs, reaching down to pull up the dress. It gives him access, along with a cool ruffle of air against my stomach. My matching gold panties—a thong, really, so the line wouldn't show in the dress—come off with a snap of expensive fabric. "I'll give you what you need, you selfish girl. I'll take care of you. Let go, sweetheart. Let go."

His fingers find my clit. He makes me ready until I'm mindless. Begging. Humping his hand. Sending a long line of arousal down the inside of my thigh.

Then there's a break. The cut of a circuit. He pulls away long enough to free himself.

He turns me around, so I'm facing the walls. His hands enclose mine from the back, placing them on the concrete. It feels like dust-covered gloss. Like I could slip, if I don't dig in my nails. His hands are sure as they lift my ass.

A pause. I can feel the weight of his gaze on my ass.

He covers me with his body.

"I wish I could memorize this," he says, murmuring in my ear.

Anyone could say it. It wouldn't be foreboding. Anyone could say it, but it's not anyone who presses his cock inside me. It's Finn. It's the man I love, fucking me as if we only have hours left instead of days, instead of years. Instead of a lifetime.

Chapter Ten

Finn

IN THE AFTERMATH, sweat dries on my body, leaving me cold. After straightening our clothes, I take off my jacket and put it around her shoulders. It makes her look small and vulnerable, the tux from my larger body on her slender frame.

She looks dazed and sex-drenched. There's no way I'm taking her back through the ballroom or even the kitchens. No other man gets to see her like this, orgasm softening her fierceness until she's pouring out, radiating, a soft glow. I'll have to find some other, smaller exit and have the driver meet us there.

I press a kiss to her forehead, feeling protective. "You okay?"

"Why wouldn't I be?"

"Because I used you hard."

She gives me a dreamy smile. "No, I'm the one who used you."

I manage a mocking glance. "That's right. Because you're so selfish."

She's the least selfish person I've ever met in my life. It's not only the obvious things, her leadership at the Morelli Fund. Hell, its very existence is only because of her. It's also the way she loves, so completely. Irrevocably. It's tragic, really.

Selfish. Ha.

I'll give her a million orgasms. She'll store them like raindrops, creating a whole lake of memories to swim in, when I become too childlike to fuck her.

She sighs and leans against me, resting her head on my chest. "I love you, Phineas Galileo Hughes."

"And I love you, Eva…" I pause and shake my head, as if clearing away cobwebs. "I love you, too, Eva…" I falter. How can I not know it? "Eva Morelli."

"You know my middle name," she whispers.

"Of course I do. It's…"

My mind is a blank slate. What's her middle name? I know it. I have to know it. "I remembered the names of a hundred acquaintances and society connections out there. I don't even give a fuck about them, but I remembered their names. Which horses they back. Their trips to Wimbledon. Their hunting lodges in the wilds of Quebec."

"It... it doesn't matter," she says. "My middle name is—"

"No. Don't tell me. I know it. Of course I know it. I love you. You're carrying our child. We're going to get married. Of course I know what your middle name is."

Her eyes are dark pools, glinting tears. "Finn."

"You wrote it across my chest. I remember the feel of your fingertip tracing through my chest hair, the sensation that made my cock hard. I remember the warmth of your body that night. So of course I remember what letters it spelled."

She's silent in her grief now, unable to pretend.

I'm the one pretending now.

I pace away from her and put a hand on the wall. It's coming to me. Any minute now the name will slip off my tongue. Eva Something Morelli. What could it be? Eva Michelle Morelli. Eva Renee Morelli. Eva Lucinda Morelli. They're all just random hollow sounds. They could be right, and I might not even know, though most likely they're wrong. Names I've heard before—before I ever met her.

"I know every company in the S&P 500. I've met most of their executive teams, at some point or another. I have a standing monthly lunch date with the CEO of Nvidia. I play golf with the President of Berkshire Hathaway. I have a couple of different corporate spies on the payroll at Meta and Tesla and Microsoft, and I know all of their names."

"Are you really supposed to be admitting that?"

It's an opening, I can tell. The perfect opportunity for me to joke about how she must be familiar with the white collar warfare of corporate espionage, considering her father and her brothers do it all the time. She left me that opening on purpose, but I can't take it. I can't turn the conversation away from her middle name.

Trying to think of it just makes it harder.

It keeps slipping away, like trying to catch a breeze.

"Pi," I say, my voice rough.

"Pie?"

"I can recite pi to a hundred digits. Three point one four one five nine two six five three five eight nine seven nine two three eight four six." I spare her the rest of the recitation, instead continuing in my head. Eight nine seven nine three two three... I know them. They're correct. Somehow I know it's right; not just a random jumble.

So why can't I remember her middle name?

"It's Honorata," she blurts out, her voice trembling and loud. Afraid. She's afraid, and I can't even console her. This is happening.

What a hell it is for a man not to be able to protect his woman from himself.

"Honorata," I say, tasting the syllables. "Eva Honorata Morelli."

Now that the name hangs in the air, I remember it. It was right after I told her everything—the Hughes curse, my inevitable end, the promise I'd made to my father.

She hadn't believed it.

Excuse me if I don't believe in generational curses and old wives' tales.

Then she'd returned the secret-sharing with a gift of her middle name. That night she'd written it across my skin, branded me in a way that felt irrevocable. I was hers. And she was mine. Forever, forever. That's what it felt like, but that feeling was a lie.

This is the truth, this cold, clinking certainty.

It's happening.

The curse is happening right now. I can't stop it. That doctor outside? Dr. Faulk. And the man with her. What was his name? They work at the Tuffin Institute, I know that much. His name had started with A. Anthony. Archer. No, it had been Alistair. An old-world name.

They can't save me. No matter what happens next, no matter the outcome of the study and how much money and support the Morelli Fund gives them, it's too fucking late.

A hand on my arm. Eva looks lost and fragile. Alone.

Because she is alone.

This will be a marriage of one person, and she's finally seeing that.

"Please," she says, her voice thick with tears. "Don't let this change everything. Don't let this make you lose hope. You can forget a name. You can walk into the wrong room. It doesn't have to mean anything if you don't let it."

That's where she's right.

Because this changes nothing.

Not for me. I always knew how it would end.

It's also where she's wrong.

"I haven't lost hope, Eva Honorata Morelli," I say, taking her in my arms. "I've gained it. I believe you'll solve this—with time. You'll break the curse. Not with me, but with our child, and that is the greatest gift you could give me."

Chapter Eleven

Eva

THE OFFICE IS beautiful and upscale, the kind of place where Katy Perry and Beyoncé have their children. I started at a more ordinary doctor's office, but after the nurse spilled the news to a reporter, I had to find someplace else. Someplace with an ironclad NDA.

The first place had taupe walls and magazines spread out on the coffee table. They had posters of childbirth information with a splash of floral art.

In contrast, I walk into a bohemian paradise with low, wide chairs made of teak and flax cushioning. The wall is painted a pleasing mix of greige and deep teal. Low lighting made by paper lanterns strung up in pleasing, purposeful randomness.

It looks like someone's stylish, comfortable living room.

Or maybe a coffee shop.

The expansive beverage offerings don't hurt with that. There's a complicated espresso machine that the secretary knows how to use for the patients, along with tall containers of ice water with strawberries and basil mixed in, which pours from an antique gold spout.

Little jars contain nuts and granola in case we're hungry while we wait.

I'm not hungry, though. Or thirsty.

I'm tense, because things have been subdued between me and Finn. We didn't talk much when we got back from the charity gala. He slept at my place. He was even more solicitous than usual, taking care of me with deliberate gentleness—as if I needed it.

Maybe I did need it.

The sex at the gala had been scorching hot. Incredible. And heartbreaking by the end, when he couldn't remember my middle name. I couldn't laugh it off the way I could the closet thing at my loft. We've talked about our middle names before, early and relatively often. He's whispered it at tenderly sensual moments, not even pausing to think, as if it were second nature.

As if it were a prayer. And then last night? Nothing.

Could it be a random thing?

Of course. We'll never know. There's no way to know.

So here we are, living in a grim new reality. No, that's not quite true. It's always been his reality. His parents told him how it would end from the time he was a toddler. The only person surprised by the dangerous fracture of hope? Me.

"I'm so sorry," the nurse says with an apologetic smile. Instead of the usual scrubs made in bright colors, she's wearing a beige fitted blouse that looks more stylish than most clothes. Only the matching beige pants, form fitting with a slight flare, make it clear that it's a uniform. "Dr. Hoffman had a delivery early this morning, and it's a long labor. We could reschedule or we could fit you in with one of our other doctors?"

"Oh, no problem," I say, stalling as I try to think of the answer. One of the things I love about Dr. Hoffman is that she insists on attending every one of her patient's births. I heard from my cousin that it's not always the case. She saw her first OB-GYN for the full nine months. Then when she went into labor at 1 a.m. it was some random doctor at the hospital who delivered her child. One who wasn't familiar with her birth plan and didn't care. One who kept ordering interventions even though her labor was progressing fine. For her second child she'd opted for a midwife and a home birth.

I'm not quite brave enough to go for that, but I am nervous about working with new people. Then again, it's only one visit. And if I'm going to request that a doctor drop everything to attend my birth, it only makes sense that sometimes she'd be unavailable for my appointments, too.

What finally decides me, though, is the rigamarole required to get us here. Building security needed to be alerted. Finn's security team had handled that, with Leo looking over his shoulder, metaphorically speaking. We'd needed special permission for a guard to accompany us. Our only concession is that he's standing outside, in the hallway, looking conspicuous as hell, as if he's guarding a private poker game instead of a doctor's office.

I really want to know the gender of the baby, and I don't want to have to do all this again in a few days. Only to discover that she's attending another delivery.

"I'll see whoever's available," I say, nodding.

"Are you sure?" Finn asks, his voice low.

"Of course it's fine," I say, overly bright. I don't want him to worry.

"That's wonderful," the nurse says, giving a bright smile and a playful wink. "You'll adore Dr. Walker. All of his patients do. He has a way with the ladies."

"Oh." I blink, uncertain what to think about a man doing my exam. I've only ever had women gynecologists. Maybe I'm traditional that way. I don't think it's wrong for other people, of course. I'm just not that comfortable with strange men. Especially older men, where they're in a position of power and prominence. It reminds me too much of my first relationship.

Then again, he's a professional.

I'm overthinking this.

I follow the nurse down the hallway, feeling Finn's hand on my lower back.

She shows us into the exam room, which looks more like a massage room at a high-end spa. There's an antique divider for me to change behind, a plush white robe to wear during the exam, and a beige-sheet-covered table.

Only the stirrups give away its purpose.

Finn takes a seat in the armchair for that purpose, and I go behind the divider to undress. Then he's standing again as I hop onto the seat, always the gentleman, helping me onto the stool so I can hop up. It's always a strange position, this. Like being on stage. Which would be nerve-wracking under any situation, but being on stage without panties? With a stranger? I miss Dr. Hoffman. She's always kind and frank and slightly funny, so it puts me at ease.

Then again, Dr. Walker works with her. They probably have similar bedside manners. And the nurse had seemed to think I'd like this guy.

Not that it really matters.

It's only one visit.

"Hello, hello," says a man with a booming voice and a bright, overly white smile. Veneers, definitely. He's handsome, with a bearing that says he knows it. "So lovely to meet you, Ms. Morelli. I took the liberty of reviewing your chart, and I'm honored that I get to do the gender reveal. Yes? No? We want to find out the sex of the baby?"

"Yes," I say, laughing a little, nervous.

There's something a little… surface about this guy, but I don't want to make it a thing. Despite the strange anxiety bumping away in the pit of my stomach. Or maybe that's the baby. Right now he or she is the size of a banana, according to the app that I use to track the progress.

The doctor claps his hands together, making me jump. "Absolutely. This is going to be fun. Relax," he says, noticing my tension. "This won't hurt a bit."

He puts a hand on my knee, as if comforting me.

I don't like it.

Beside me, I feel Finn tense. Maybe someone else couldn't feel it. They definitely couldn't see it. His handsome face looks expressionless, but compared to his usual charm it's a stark contrast. The last thing I need is for an argument to break out before I find out the gender.

"Let's get started," I say.

"Eager girl," the doctor says with a chuckle, and Finn's eyes narrow.

My fiancé stands, appearing somehow more imposing. "Dr. Wallis."

"Walker."

"Whatever. Please show my fiancée the respect any patient deserves."

Even though the doctor is taller, Finn is more fierce. More determined. More real, in every way. It infuses the room. It's like watching two wolves face off, ears down, teeth bared, hair bristling.

As I watch, Dr. Walker becomes visibly smaller. He clears his throat and sits on the rolling stool, cowed. "Yes, of course. My apologies for my… casual manner."

The physical exam happens in a brusque, professional manner. There's nothing suggestive about the way he touches me. It's about the same as Dr. Hoffman, if a little less gentle. "Everything looks good here," he says, taking off a glove with a loud *snap*. "Now I'll send the ultrasound technician in. And once she's done, we'll go over the results."

Chapter Twelve

Eva

As soon as he leaves the room, I let out a breath of relief.

"I should have rescheduled," Finn says on a growl.

"No," I say, putting a hand on his arm. "There was no need for that. And it wasn't your decision to make. It was mine. I'm the pregnant lady here."

"That's why I kept my mouth shut, but now I regret it. The guy's a prick."

I don't really disagree, though he did nothing directly wrong. It's just a feeling, but I learned to follow my feelings a long time ago. I should have spoken up, or at least allowed Finn to advocate for me. I'm so used to being the strong one, the fixer. I'm so used to solving everyone else's problems and keeping my mouth shut when I have one of my own. Having someone on my side, an ally, a soon-to-be husband, is still a new idea.

"Let's not think about him," I say. "I'm so excited about the ultrasound."

He doesn't respond, and I know why.

"Come on," I say, gently cajoling. "We don't know what the gender is, not really."

A dark glance. "We do."

Because part of the Hughes curse is that the main line can only produce boys. Supposedly. It seems like a bit of folklore. Even if early-onset dementia runs in the family, even if boys are genetically more likely, it doesn't mean that a girl is impossible.

Not that I'd mind a boy.

In fact I'd love to hold a miniature Finn, with dark blond hair and hazel eyes, with an irreverent grin and a thirst for adventure. He'd be handful, but I would love it, love him, just as much as I'd love a girl.

It's not that I'd mind a boy. It's just that, a little bit, it would be a confirmation of the Hughes curse. As if it would prove the inevitability of their disease. As if it's some supernatural hex, rather than a happenstance of genetics.

If it was a girl, I think Finn would believe the

curse was broken.

And that would be powerful.

The ultrasound tech is a bubbly young woman named Halsey, "no relation to the singer, my friends call me Hals, and you can, too!" She walks me through the process of the ultrasound with the patience and genuine consideration I expect from Dr. Hoffman.

"Now if it's a boy, we'll be able to tell," Hals says, "on account of his knickknack, but a girl, there's more of a chance for error, since it might be a trick of the position."

"Got it," I say, tensing as she puts the gel on my stomach. It's warm, which I appreciate, but still an uneasy sensation. "Knickknack? That's a new one."

Hals giggles. "I make up a new term every time I do the ultrasound. The whiz bang. The thingamajig. The green eggs and ham."

That makes me laugh, despite myself. "The green eggs and ham?"

Even Finn quirks a smile. "The pocket watch," he suggests.

"The orange peel," I say, making them both laugh.

"Please no," Finn says, teasing. "I can live with an orange, but not the peel."

"I'm going to use that one next time," Hals says cheerfully.

She takes a little time setting up the machine. There's white and black movement on the screen, broad strokes, unintelligible, at least to me. Finally she settles around a few particular black and white blobs. The sound of a heartbeat fills the room, and I meet Finn's warm gaze.

"That's him," he says, sounding reverent.

"Or her," I say.

It doesn't matter. I keep repeating that to myself, but I'm not sure I believe it. Without the curse, either a boy or a girl would be lovely. But it would be so great if a girl could definitively break the curse, if Finn could believe in that.

"Let's see if we can find that orange peel," Hals says, her eyes trained on the screen as her hand moves the wand expertly through the gel on my baby bump.

She squints and leans closer to the screen. "Aha! There it is."

"It's a boy?" I ask, breathless and jittery.

"It's a boy," she says, beaming. She proceeds to point out a few of the white areas—a leg, a stomach, and a very small speck of white that apparently is his orange peel. None of it really looks like a baby, but the heartbeat thrumming through the room proves it is.

A boy.

I love everything about a boy. Trains, planes, and automobiles. Rough and tumble. A puppy as a sidekick as they have adventures outside. I can already envision him building forts in the backyard. Or maybe he'll be a boy with softer pursuits. Playing make believe with legos and helping to make pretend food in the kitchen and drawing stories on the walls.

I'll love him however he is, but…

It does feel, despite my best efforts, like a confirmation.

That the Hughes curse is real.

I believe in magic, I told the people from the Tuffin Institute. I believe in miracles. Not because I'm anti-science. Not even because I'm religious though I attend mass with Leo often. It's because there are things that science doesn't yet explain. There *is* a reason, we just haven't figured it out yet. What if this is like that? What if the curse—the steady stream of boys, the inevitable and quick descent into dementia—is inescapable?

Thump, thump, thump.

This baby doesn't know about the curse.

He might not even be affected by it… but he probably is.

THREE TO GET READY

I can't deny that any longer. Whether it's ordinary genetics having their way or something more esoteric, it's feeling more and more likely.

With Finn forgetting my middle name.

With the baby being a boy.

With the pounding in my chest.

Hals holds the ultrasound wand steady as she clicks on the other end of the machine. Little cross hatches and lines are drawn across the white blobs, along with measurements.

There's a movement inside. Not a movement made by me. Not a movement made by her. I can't even feel it inside my tummy, but I can *see* it in the ultrasound, the flutter and shift of the baby. A tiny being who can't see or speak. A boy who's reliant on me fully.

Will he be afraid when he finds out about the curse?

Will he resent me for bringing him into the world?

I've never considered an abortion for him, and I'm not considering it now, but it still makes me wonder. The way Finn talks about it, sometimes I wonder if he'd rather his parents made a different choice. The idea seems anathema to my very being. No matter how badly things got at home, even when my heart broke from the betrayal of

Lane Constantine, I valued life above everything. Even pain. Even heartache. Even dementia, if I had thought of it.

That was before I knew about it, though.

Before I'd really understood or thought deeply about what it means.

Becoming a child when everyone else stays an adult.

Being dependent on your family for getting dressed, for bathing, for using the bathroom.

Alzheimer's is a broken record, playing the same song on repeat. It's a cacophony so loud and jarring that it makes you feel like you're going insane. It's a ticking clock, an incessant chime. It's an infinite number of sounds, all of them lonely.

That's the ending I've consigned this baby to live.

The baby moves again, innocent and contented in my womb.

He doesn't know.

He isn't afraid, because he doesn't know.

Thump, thump, thump.

His heartbeat sounds strong. Hopeful.

Except I'm not hopeful anymore. I'm heartbroken.

All of it comes together in a blinding, grievous panic: the complicated ethics of procreation, the primal certainty that I'll lose the people I love the most. The knowledge that I'm not enough, I'm never enough to save them from the very worst.

Fear drenches me, leaving me cold and sweaty at the same time.

My breath comes faster and faster, and then not at all. I gasp out, but it feels like I'm strangling. The baby. Finn. My parents. My brothers and sisters. Finn's father and brother. His mother. Everyone who relies on Hughes Industries. Everyone we've ever helped with the Morelli Fund, and everyone we *could* help in some distant future. All of them slipping through my fingers; I can't catch them. I can't help them. I can't save them.

I can't even save myself.

That's the shameful truth.

"Are you okay?" Halsey's voice comes from far away.

"Eva." It's Finn. Steady, calm, strong Finn. He's been dealing with this fear since he was five years old—and it wasn't only about himself. His father. His brother.

Tears leak down my cheeks. It isn't a heavy gust of a cry, but a dense fog.

"I'm going to get Dr. Walker."

"No," Finn says. "Don't. Give us a few

minutes alone."

My stomach is wiped free of the goop and my robe readjusted. I'm trembling. Dimly I'm aware of Finn's hands on me, gentle and coaxing. Patient, as well. He rubs slow circles around my back, leaning me forward so I'm not reclined and feeling helpless.

I press my hands to my face, which feels abnormally hot.

"Take a deep breath."

I focus on Finn's voice.

"Good. Another."

He coaxes me back to awareness, where every muscle feels like it's a wet cloth that's been wrung out. "I'm sorry," I mumble. "Sorry."

"Don't apologize. Anyone would be upset."

He knows. He knows why I had a panic attack so soon after learning the baby's a boy. It's confirmation of a reality that he's always known as fact. He doesn't say, *I told you so.* Phineas Hughes would never be so crass. I'm the one who thinks it. He told me so.

He knew.

I'm the one who's been spinning stories in my head.

When I was pursued by a married man who told me all sorts of lies. He said his marriage was a sham, that he'd leave his wife for me. That he loved me. And I was so used to taking care of everyone, my family, my siblings—even as a child, I took care of them—that the idea of having an older, powerful man shelter me felt almost addictive.

I could be excused, I suppose, for being young and foolish in the face of a far more experienced lover. One well-versed in the lies of seduction.

It never should have happened again, though.

I spun fairy tales in the clouds, and somehow, somehow, I've done it again.

Chapter Thirteen

Finn

As soon as we arrive home, I know something's wrong.

There are a couple of extra cars pulled in the circular drive. In particular the black Lexus with the New Jersey plates belongs to Dr. Ranier, my father's primary physician. He comes once a week to see how he's doing, routine visits where nothing much changes. Those visits happen on Wednesday mornings, not on Friday in the late evening.

Eva senses my mood. "What's going on?"

"It's Dad."

That's all I have to say. She's quiet and quick as she follows me inside. I don't bother parking in the garage; it's quicker to go in this way.

We decided not to stay at her loft tonight

because the doctor's office is closer to Bishop's Landing. And I don't have to go into the office tomorrow.

Plus, I've been spending less time with my father.

He has Hemingway and my mother now, but it's not the same.

Now it might be too late.

We're at the front door when we hear the strident whine of an ambulance. It turns the corner, and my heartbeat races. What the hell happened?

"Go," Eva says, her expression calm and competent. "I'll direct them inside."

I don't even have time for thanks. I run through the house and take the back stairs two at a time. And find absolute chaos. The doctor is there, and two of his nurses. They surround his bed, doing something I don't immediately recognize, adjusting and fussing.

Along with my mother, crying.

It's Hemingway who's clear eyed enough to answer me.

"He fell," he says, his voice grim. "Doctor says he might have broken something."

"Fuck." He might have broken several somethings. "Where?"

A pause. Then, "The gazebo outside."

"What the fuck was he doing there?"

"I don't know." Hemingway raises his chin, as if facing down a firing squad. "It's my fault, though. I should have known something was off during dinner. He kept talking about sailing and the water and the feel of the breeze. Don't blame Mom."

I look at our mother, who's sitting in an armchair with a shattered expression and tears tracking down her cheeks. Most people assume they're estranged, that it's a typical society marriage gone stale, since she travels the world in a never-ending tour.

I know different.

Because I saw how they were before. In love.

True fucking love, for all the good it did them.

That's why I avoided real relationships before Eva. Not because I didn't believe in them. It was because I knew the paradise that could be lost.

"Why would I blame her?" I ask, forcing myself to some semblance of calm.

"She was—" He looks away, as if unable to finish.

A cold feeling runs through me. "She was what?"

"She was sleeping in his room, okay? She dismissed the nurse. He was having a lucid moment at the dinner table. They talked about the way they used to go sailing." The tips of Hemingway's ears turn pink. "And then they kissed. I... immediately left."

Hell. A moment of lucidity. Ironic that it should have been the cause of disaster.

Hemingway blushing about our mother's show of affection is so normal it's adorable.

Our family isn't normal.

I never blamed her for leaving Dad. It would be like living in Antarctica for their temperate summers. They were nice for the handful of days they lasted, and pure hell the rest. Sometimes, in my darker moments, I blamed her for leaving Hemingway. And me.

But this? Fuck.

I make my way over to my father. He's incoherent, mumbling something about water and moonlight. He doesn't appear to be in pain, but that's almost more scary. The nurse stands aside to allow me in. The usually unflappable Dr. Ranier looks distressed.

"I had to sedate him," he says.

"That's why he doesn't seem like he's in pain."

"No, it's… I'm concerned about his state of mind. They say they found him still trying to get up to go sailing. That he fought them as they tried to get him inside."

Fear makes my blood freeze. What if he'd made it to the water? He'd be dead right now. He would have drowned. Even if muscle memory had kicked in and he remembered how to swim, he couldn't have swam forever. Not to mention that it's cold outside.

He bats at the nurse's hands ineffectually, trying to get up.

"Dad," I say, leaning over him. "It's me. Finn. Phineas."

"Want to go sailing, Finny boy. Want to sail around the cape and back again."

"We will, Dad. Promise. Just focus on getting better."

"Feel fine," he mumbles, his eyes hazy.

There's a commotion behind me as the paramedics come in. I move out of the way along with everyone else. Dr. Ranier passes on the salient medical information—the nature of his fall, his current health condition, the medications he's on. I'm useless in this tableau.

"Why didn't you call me?" I ask Hemingway.

He shakes his head. "There was no time. And

I thought—"

"You didn't want to bother me."

"I knew you were at the doctor's office with Eva. And you couldn't do anything here. We could have loaded him into the ambulance. I was planning to drive to the hospital behind him and then text you when you got home."

"God fucking damn it, Hemingway."

He throws up his hands. "What could you have done if you were here? Not that you could have driven home any faster in the middle of rush hour. So... what? You would have just worried and freaked out while in traffic?"

"That's my *right*."

"Well, it doesn't seem very useful. Or safe."

"I want to know when something happens to him. I need to be informed. I can't—"

"Finn." He puts his hands on my shoulders, squaring off with me, his blue gaze intense. "I know you're used to shouldering everything in this family, but I'm older now. Grown. You were the same age I am right now when you took over Hughes Industries."

Eva appears at the top of the stairs as a whir of the ambulance kicks off from outside. She looks calm and resolute. This is a woman who's had entirely too much experience handling emergencies. Fucking unfair that she's marrying into a family with more of them.

"Christ. I'm sorry I snapped," I say to Hemingway. "I still don't like it, but I hear what you're saying. Mostly I'm just worried and taking it out on you like an asshole."

He gives me a firm nod. "I'm going to drive Mom to the hospital. You can take Eva. That way if we need to bring them back early we'll have two cars."

He heads downstairs to pull the car around from the garage.

Eva joins me, leaning into my side with gentle support.

"When the hell did he become an adult?" I say, staring after him.

A soft smile. "He makes a good one."

Yeah, he managed some pretty clear thinking for a disaster.

And he even managed me and my temper.

Eva isn't the only person in the room here with too much experience handling them.

"We're going to follow them to the hospital," I tell her, placing a grateful kiss on her forehead. "Thank you for this. For everything. I just need a minute."

I go to my mother and crouch in front of her.

Slowly, slowly, she focuses on me. "Finn?"

"Yeah, Mom." My voice is hoarse. "You okay?"

Her head shakes slowly, but the desolate expression in her eyes says it all. "Some people wish, you know. They pray. They want one more day with the people they loved, but I know better. One day is worse than nothing. To have him back and then lose him again."

"I know."

"I'm sorry," she says. "I didn't mean to fall asleep."

"You don't have to apologize."

Her lower lip trembles. "Yes. I do. For tonight and for every night before this one, not being here, making you bear the weight of this. For falling in love with him in the first place. For making you and Hemingway live this curse. God, you must hate me."

I glance back at Eva.

It's the same fear she had at the doctor's office, that the baby is a mistake.

A year ago I would have agreed with her.

Now, I'm not so sure.

That small bump? Those black and white shadows? The steady rhythm of his heart? I already love him, this tiny, unnamed child.

And how can you regret love? You can't.

Not really.

You can run from it.

You can hide.

God knows I tried both of those things.

You can fight all you want, but love has its way.

And in the end, it's worth living for.

It's the only thing that is.

Chapter Fourteen

Eva

My fingers entwine with Finn's as we hurry through the whooshing automatic doors into the antiseptic-scented lobby. It's full. Every seat in the waiting area taken, with many setup along the wall. A few people are in wheelchairs that appear to be provided by the hospital, thick blue metal piping with a handle on the back like it's a shopping cart.

Another man has a more traditional wheelchair, presumably his own, with two amputated legs. There's no one around him, no wife or child comforting him, and he's shouting. The people seated around him seem oblivious, so presumably it's been happening for some time.

One mother has created makeshift sleeping bags for her two small children in a corner.

Half of the people are coughing.

Someone holds a bloodied bandage to their temple.

There's only one receptionist for a waiting area that must hold a hundred people.

It's such a contrast to the gynecologist's office I was in only hours ago.

Of course, some of that is due to the fact that it was for regular visits, whereas this is for emergencies. An ER is bound to be more busy, more chaotic, and more depressing than a regular doctor's office. But it's more than that. It's about class differences. And for some people, an emergency room trip is the only time they ever see a doctor.

At the desk, a nurse directs us through the wide double doors.

She presses a button, which causes them to open, and we walk through.

Because Finn's father's fall was serious enough to warrant immediate care, bypassing the line ahead of all these people? Maybe so. I've heard falls can be absolutely terrible for older people. And emergency rooms are run on a triage system, with the most severe cases treated first, regardless of the order in which you arrive.

Then again, it could be that he's getting better

care because of who he is.

Because of the zip code where the ambulance picked him up.

Either way, we're shown into a deeper waiting area, this one slightly less crowded. This one doesn't appear to have patients, only waiting family members like us.

"Will you be okay?" Finn asks.

I reach up on my tiptoes and kiss his cheek. "Of course."

He leaves to go find more information about his father's condition.

And probably do some more of that Finn Hughes magic, such as making sure they call in the best surgeon. Also to get security, because the sad truth is, there are people in the world who would try to capitalize on this event. Pictures of one of the wealthiest men in America on a stretcher would sell for a lot of money.

Hemingway settles near the window, looking out over a small courtyard with trees and cobblestone. Geneva sits in one of the chairs, looking shell-shocked. I order some coffee from the vending machine, waiting while it sends a small stream of brown liquid into a Styrofoam cup.

I offer it to her, but she shakes her head no.

So I take a sip and immediately regret it, coughing.

That makes a smile ghost her lips.

I sit down next to her, wondering if I can possibly offer comfort to this woman. Wondering if she even wants me to try. We aren't friends. We might even be enemies. After all, her sister is Caroline Constantine, wife to the man I had an affair with years ago.

Though I don't know if she knows that.

I'm also marrying her son against her advice.

And pregnant out of wedlock. Perhaps not that shocking in this modern age, especially considering we're engaged, but the Hughes are an old-money family. Established and highborn and well-mannered. I'm also a couple years older than Finn.

"I love him, you know."

"Finn?"

"Daniel. But yes, I love Finn, too. Daniel was so proud when he was born. He was so happy to have a son, even knowing what would become of him. It didn't seem to bother him, keeping the curse going."

I make a small sound, almost involuntary.

She shakes her head, as if mystified. "And I thought… God, I don't know what I thought. It almost seemed like our love could conquer anything."

Half wondering if she'll rebuff me, I reach over to take her hand.

Her eyes meet mine, and then she squeezes. "I appreciate what you're doing with Finn, you know. Even though I said you should leave, I didn't mean it." A chagrined smile. "Well, I did mean it. I thought you could save yourself, but I see the way you look at him. You already loved him, even then. It was too late. By the time you're in love it's too late."

"Too late for what?" I find myself asking.

I should probably keep my mouth shut, considering this woman will be my mother-in-law. The grandmother of my child. Considering she's dealing with grief and fear right now, but I can't stay quiet. Not when she keeps lamenting something that most people wish they could experience. Tinder and blind dates and a thousand other ways that people struggle to find connection. She had it. For however short of a time, it was hers.

"Would you go back and undo it all, if you could? Take away your love, your happiness? Take away your sons? Erase them from the earth?"

Her eyebrows rise. Her lips purse, and she

reminds me of her sister, Caroline, of the severe look she gets before delivering a cutting public setdown. Then she shakes her head, as if losing her will to fight. "I wouldn't take it back, not a single second. That doesn't make it any easier to bear, this long, slow descent into death. I experience the grieving process again and again. Every year. Every month. And ten times tonight."

I swallow hard. "I'm sorry."

Our hands are still linked, and she squeezes. "You're good for Finn. And stronger than I ever was. Strong enough to bear the weight of the Hughes curse, if anyone is."

"Strong enough to break it?"

She gives a soft, unsteady laugh. "If anyone can, darling, it's you."

"But you don't believe it will happen."

A pause. "No. I've lived too long under its shadow to imagine a world without it, but maybe that's why we have children. Maybe that's why we bring them into this world, full of chaos and violence, full of tragedy, because they can imagine something better."

Chapter Fifteen

Finn

MERCY HOSPITAL'S BEST surgeon on call, Neha Khan, smells faintly of stale beer and French fries. A pub on Friday night, I'm assuming. She's wearing fresh scrubs and a severe expression as she talks to the nurse. My father's being prepped for the operation room. Dr. Khan is on her way inside, but she's going to talk to me first.

"You're the son," she asks, washing her hands and arms until they turn red in a big industrial sink. "And rich. The hospital administrator called me himself."

"What's happening with my father?"

She spouts off some medical speak with words like *femoral neck fracture* and *pinning*.

"Tell it to me like I'm not a doctor."

"He broke his hip, Mr. Hughes. In multiple places. That's a serious injury. And the sooner I get in there, the sooner I can work on it. Best case scenario, I reconstruct the bones using plates and screws."

"And worst case?"

"Worst case we're looking at a hip replacement."

"What does that mean? Recovery-wise?"

"You're looking at a long road, Mr. Hughes. It's not like breaking an arm when you're a kid. The hip? It's at the core of the body. Right now, I'm focused on repairing his hip, but even if we're successful, it will be a hard road. Some doctors won't tell you the truth, but I'd rather the families be prepared. Fifty percent of people who go through this die within six months."

The news hits me like a physical blow.

I've been so fucking worried about his memory loss, about grieving the mental part of him. And now I might lose the physical part, too. "I want to talk to him."

"Unless you know how to use a scalpel, you're no use to him."

"Humor me."

She stops what she's doing and looks at me. "You're not used to being told no, are you?"

"Not when it's about my family."

A nod. "Then scrub in. If you're going to keep talking, you're going to have to come inside the operating room. And in order to do that, I need you sterile."

A few minutes later I'm wearing a blue covering over my clothes and a green scrub cap on my hair. It occurs to me that I look like a father in the delivery room.

This isn't a delivery room.

It's not about bringing a new life into the room. It's about saving one.

She nods toward the bed in the center of the room. "You have exactly six minutes."

Lights are shining on him, overbright in an already well-lit room. It makes him seem like he's glowing. I stand by his head. His eyelids open, revealing hazel eyes like my own.

"Hi, Dad."

"Finny boy." His voice is raspy and slow. They've given him better drugs than Dr. Ranier. It's taken away that edge of anxiety. Now his hands rest at his side. He looks at me with a serene expression.

I'm not sure he knows what's happening to him.

It's probably better that he doesn't.

"You remember your promise, don't you?"

My throat burns. "Yeah."

A small spark of awareness lights in his eyes. As if he's really there, looking back at me, the same way he did many years ago. Daniel Hughes. Business man. Loyal husband. Caring father. "You kept it?"

I take his hand, which feels papery and cold, and link our pinkies together. "Promise."

A nod, and then he closes his eyes.

Chapter Sixteen

Finn, many years ago

Water slaps against the hull with more strength than you'd expect it to have.

It's different than when you're sailing at twenty knots. The bow breaking through the waves. Even when it's choppy water, when it feels like you're going to bounce right off the deck, there's a certain rhythm to it. *Thud thud thud.* Fast, almost like bullets in an action movie, one right after the other.

But when the boat stands still, the ocean bats it around in an uneven way, like a cat playing with a mouse. It rocks me this way and that, and my sea legs, as Daddy calls them, go away.

I stagger across the deck and sit down on the blanket.

Daddy's already there, leaning back, hands

behind his head.

He's watching the stars, so I try to watch them, too, even though they aren't as exciting as the satellite TV that could play inside the cockpit. That's why we come out here at night. A boat ride can be a lot of different ways. First thing in the morning for some fishing. Snorkeling in the afternoon. I like all of them, even this one, the one where we lie down and look at the stars, because it's just me and him.

"Canis Major," he says.

That's an easy one, because it has the brightest star. I point. "There."

"Gemini."

I find Castor and Pollux, the two bright ones. They're supposed to be twins, which I think is mostly because people didn't have satellite TV back then. "There."

"Aries," he says, and I look for the ram that doesn't look anything like a ram.

It looks like a bend. A boomerang, maybe. Sometimes Mom comes on these, and she lets me make up my own constellations, but Daddy likes the real ones. I point. "There."

A grunt that means *correct*. "And what did the ram do that was so special?"

"It made the Golden Fleece."

"Which is…?"

"Only for kings. Jason had to find the Golden Fleece to claim his rightful throne."

"He didn't do it alone, did he?"

"He was helped by Medea, his wife."

"Good," he says, sounding pleased with me.

I smile even though he can't see me. Or maybe because he can't see me.

When he's proud of me it doesn't matter as much that we eat cans of tuna fish for dinner or that I'm always so sleepy the next morning. I'd go on a thousand nighttime boat rides.

"You know why I named you Galileo, right, Finny boy?"

"He was an astronomer."

"That's right. He discovered that the world went around the sun, instead of the other way around. But people didn't like that. The church in particular. They wanted to believe what they wanted to believe, and they threatened him, you understand? They put him in jail and threatened to kill him if he kept speaking the truth."

I shiver as the night air brushes over my face. "The church?"

"They were the people in power back then, but it's the same now, really. People in charge who don't want to know the truth. He had to recant—that means to take it back. He had to lie and say that the earth didn't *really* go around the sun in order to live."

I'm silent, because I don't know the right answer. This isn't one of the constellation stories like Jason and the Argonauts that I've memorized.

"Do you understand what I'm saying?" Daddy asks.

Disappointment makes my stomach hurt. "No."

"The lie? That was his Golden Fleece. That's what he needed to take his rightful place." He laughs, but it doesn't sound like his other laughs. "That's what they don't tell you. The Golden Fleece isn't money or power or even truth. It's a lie."

He turns to face me, his eyes dark in the night.

"There will come a time when you need to lie, Finny boy. Understand? People say lying is wrong, but they don't know about the Golden Fleece. You're going to have to lie to take your rightful place. Say you understand. Promise me you'll do it."

"I promise," I say, too fast because I don't really know what I'm promising.

He sighs. "The world is changing, but not fast

enough. Not far enough. Maybe it won't ever be. Hell, it will change you, too. You'll want to do things different."

"No, I won't. I promise."

He looks at me again, considering.

"Pinky promise," I say, holding out my pinky.

"You'll lie when you have to," he says, "to save your own life. And mine. Won't you?"

Fear makes my heart beat faster. It *thud thud thuds* in an uneven rhythm, just like the waves that slap the hull. "Pinky promise."

He takes his pinky—bigger than mine—and we shake that way.

Then he's proud again. He doesn't say it, but I can see it in his face.

He lies back down on the blanket, and I do, too.

"Orion," he says, and I point.

CHAPTER SEVENTEEN

Eva

I'M STILL SITTING with Geneva Hughes, holding hands. She talks only occasionally, telling me about her husband—before she lost him. That's how she sounds. But it's less bitter now than it was when I first met her at the Hughes mansion. More wistful.

Like the time he'd ordered a hot air balloon for their one-year anniversary. The company had flown it right into their expansive back lawn, all glimmering, itchy heat. Being a typical man, she said, he'd insisted he could fly the thing with minimal instructions.

That's how they ended up heading into the sea with no idea how to get back down.

It had taken a rescue balloon to get them back down.

THREE TO GET READY

Which should have been annoying. Proof that men were too stubborn for their own good, but instead Geneva had found it exhilarating. She'd leaned over the side of the thick basket, letting the wind whip around her. It didn't matter where they were going, she said, when they were that high off the ground. It didn't matter if they'd ever even land.

That's what love does to you, she said, sounding rueful.

Now she's quiet, staring into blank space, probably reliving more memories.

Hemingway can't seem to sit down, so he's taken to pacing the floor. Occasionally he passes by and gives us updates on what he calls the budding romance between Exam Rooms 5 and 6, where a woman shouted, "Do you know the muffin man?" like the scene in the movie Shrek, and the man across the hall had yelled, "The muffin man?" To which the woman had yelled back in perfect angst, "The muffin man!"

There's movement in the hallway.

It's not Hemingway, though.

Finn appears wearing his regular clothes, a business suit that he put on for the office this morning, before he left early for the OB-GYN appointment. And for some reason, he also has a green cap tied around his head. And his eyes, those beautiful hazel eyes—sometimes soulful, sometimes playful—are filled with a new height of intensity.

Did something happen? He doesn't look sad, precisely, but he doesn't look relieved, either. Is the news about his father bad? Is he in critical condition? Or worse, has he… died? Anything seems possible with the primal energy in the room. It pulses with life and death knowledge.

Geneva hasn't seen him. He's standing outside her field of vision, unmoving.

I squeeze her hand. "I'll go look around for some better coffee," I say.

I'm not sure why I lie, except that if the worst has happened, I want to give her the extra moments of peace. Well, not peace precisely. But not complete loss, either.

She nods absently and lets go of my hand.

I circle her and meet Finn in the hallway.

Without a word he wraps his arms around me, holding me tight. I allow myself to be held; I hold him back, just as hard. There's no room for air in my lungs, but that doesn't matter as much as this embrace. Nothing matters as much as this embrace.

Then he's stalking down the hall, pulling me

alongside him, his arm around my waist. He's a man on a mission, and my breathless, half-formed questions don't land. *What's happening? Is Daniel okay? Are the doctors operating on him?*

No answer.

Which probably means something bad, so I don't push for a response.

We go down an echoing staircase and push through a heavy glass door. Then we're in the courtyard I saw from upstairs with its manicured bushes and oak trees and cobblestone. Concrete benches provide rest for the weary. The physically weary, including some nurses and doctors in scrubs. The soul-weary, including patients and families of patients.

There are only a few people here now, bowing to the cold and dark.

Through the windows someone plays a piano.

I do a double take. No, the piano looks like a regular grand piano, black and glossy, but it has some kind of mechanism that plays itself. The keys and pedals are moving, even though no one sits at the bench. Unless, of course, the hospital is haunted.

Which, of course it would be. I'm not sure why they always show haunted houses, when what's really going to be haunted is a hospital where people die every day.

Then Finn is turning me, grasping me, kissing me like I've never been kissed before.

We've had a thousand kisses.

Slow ones like a lazy summer day, sweet with honey and tanged like lemonade.

Desperate ones when we're both hungry for each other.

Powerful ones that turn my soul inside out.

This feels different in some indefinable way, like he's trying to tell me something. It's a language, this kiss—his fierce marauding, hands cradling my face, hard body pressing me into an ancient oak. Was it here before this hospital, this tree? It feels thick behind me, while Finn becomes hard and thick in front of me, his erection pressing into my stomach. It doesn't feel sexual, though. At least not the intent of the kiss; it's more of a side effect.

Then he pulls back, breath billowing in and out of him.

It occurs to me distantly that people can see us. Not only the guy on the bench in the corner or the woman sipping a steaming cup of Starbucks in front of a memorial garden. The people inside the building, too. They can look down on us from three sides. For two people fiercely protective of their privacy it should be important, but it isn't.

Everyone else has stopped mattering.

"Finn," I say, putting a shaking hand on his cheek. "Tell me what happened."

"What happened is that I... that he..." He stops. Swallows. Tries again. "I kept my promise, Eva, and maybe it was right. Maybe it was wrong, but it's done. It's over."

For a terrible, vibrating second, I think he means our relationship. The engagement, fake and real and everything in between. *It's over.* My breath stops.

Then he continues. "Whatever debt I owed to my father, it's done. Paid in full. It wasn't only the secret, you see? I couldn't be honest with anyone while it hung over me." A hollow laugh. "I couldn't even be honest with myself. I was so fucking angry at him for making me live this that I couldn't admit I wanted it. Wanted it so fucking bad."

I shake my head, not really following, but understanding the intensity, feeling it. Blood pumps through my veins at lightning speed. Time slows down. "You want it?"

"Yeah," he breathes. "Every last moment. The good times with the laughter and the sex and the feeling like my heart is going to break my ribs down with how big it seems. And the bad ones, too. The fear and the anger. The dread. The certainty that it will go away one day, because it will. Of course it will. It's not even about the curse. It's about life. We all have a secret expiration date, and it's never pretty. Whether it's a curse—or a car crash or a heart attack."

"Or a fall on a gazebo floor," I whisper.

Finn presses his forehead to mine. "He's in surgery. His chances of making it through the surgery are good, but after—after they're… they're fucking terrible."

My heart clenches. "I'm so sorry."

"It hurt more than I thought it would. For so long I've thought… he's not there. He's not really there, the father that carried me around on his shoulders. He's not inside, or when he is, it's gone so fast, like quicksilver, a trick of the light. And if he's not really there, I don't have anything to mourn, do I?"

It's more complicated than that. It always has been. And while I don't have long experience with this particular form of complicated, I know about it in other ways. Loving my father despite the fact that he slapped me across the face when I was fifteen. Loving my mother even though she never had enough maternal warmth to light a matchstick.

Life didn't give us easy. I'm not sure it really gives anyone easy.

That feels like a mirage. An untruth.

A lie, even, the same way they accuse the Hugheses of lying in the newspaper articles.

Love doesn't fix everything, but it makes it worth fixing. "Finn."

"I'm sorry."

My heart stops. "For what?"

"For doubting us. For doubting you. For letting you believe that my feelings for you could, for even one second, be temporary. Our relationship was never, ever fake."

Tears prick my eyes, making his handsome face turn blurry. "I know."

"You're too patient, but that's what love is, right? Patient and kind."

"But not easy," I say, my throat thick with emotion.

"No." He shakes his head. "Not easy. And harder for you than most, I think. You're strong enough to handle it, though. I think that's what I saw when I asked you to leave the gala with me that first night, when I took you to the boat. Some part of me knew you were strong enough to handle this, to handle me, to handle the fucking Hughes curse."

I laugh, water and uneven. "Thought you just liked the way my ass looked in that dress."

"Like a handful," he says, heated. "Like two handfuls."

"You didn't have sex with me, then."

"I wanted to. Wanted to drag you down to the berth, to make you come again and again until you were too addicted to how I made you feel to ever leave."

That makes me blush, despite the fact that he eventually did just that.

Or maybe because of it.

"It was my idea for a fake relationship," he says. "Because even when I was lying to myself, I couldn't stand the thought of watching you walk away. It was the only way I could think to keep you—with secrets and pretenses and half measures."

"You have me," I say, feeling fierce, my voice thick.

"I'm keeping you."

He tilts my head up for a kiss that steals my breath. It leaves my knees weak, but I'm supported by this big tree. This legacy of a tree. And by Finn's strong hands. The past and the future.

None of it promised forever. It's all temporary. This kiss. This breath. This body.

Only love really lasts.

"I love you," I say between biting, panting kisses.

He groans against my lips. "Love you. Love you. Fucking love you."

I moan as he hitches me higher against the tree, pressing his erection between my legs.

"I'm not promising you forever," he gasps out, grinding and grinding. "No one can. I'm promising you now. This moment and the next. Everything I am. Everything I will be."

"Yes," I cry, as he pushes me closer to orgasm. It's too fast for me to climax. He's barely even touched me, but the emotional poignance of the emotion translates into strokes on my clit. I'm already vibrating, wrapping one leg around his waist to get closer.

"Yours," he grounds out. "I'm yours."

And then I'm flying, breaking into a thousand splintered pieces, pleasure turning me into a bursting star, leaving me floating in the dark, still courtyard, the muted piano still playing Beethoven without anyone on the bench, the night sky dark above the city.

Chapter Eighteen

Finn

When we get back to the waiting area, Hemingway's waiting for us. The tops of his ears are pink, the same way they were when he talked about our parents sleeping together.

I'm assuming that means he saw Eva and me in the courtyard.

Probably a few people did. It was dark, but still bright enough to see.

"Any news?" I ask.

He shakes his head. "Not about Dad."

That makes my eyebrows rise. "Then about what?"

He doesn't say anything, just hands us his phone. A video plays. It's shaky and dark on the screen, but it comes into focus. The courtyard. The oak tree. Me and Eva, embracing and kissing and talking in an intense, private conversation.

"Send it to Douglas," I say, referring to Douglas Karl, our family lawyer. He handles a lot of things for the Hughes family, including extended relatives. This won't be the first quasi sex tape he's gotten taken down, not that we were actually having sex. Close, though.

"Already did," Hem says.

"Let me see." Eva takes the phone and watches, her expression not revealing much. Then suddenly she laughs, the sound like a burst of spring rain on parched earth. "Send those takedown notices if you really want, but... you can barely see anything. Just two people in love, and why are we trying to hide that?"

"Eva." She orgasms in that video. That part is not clear enough to see, but I can tell. I know the exact moment her body shudders in my hold. She whimpered in my ear. The video is taken from maybe one story above, half-blocked by the branches of the tree.

"Leo will throw a fit. So will my dad." She throws up her hands. "But look at us. We're in the hospital because your dad fell. That's what I care about. I'm not worried about a video where I'm being kissed by the father of my child. Like, yes, he's a great kisser. I'll go on national TV and tell everyone that, if they really want to know."

Hell. She's right. I care about what the public thinks... because my father did.

The truth is, they can go to hell.

I take her into my arms, this time in more of a G-rated hold, even though there's no one else in the hallway. "You're wonderful, you know that? A surprise. A revelation."

"God," she says, teasing. "I hope no one hears you praise me."

I lean down and whisper exactly what I think about her breasts, how luscious they are, how delicious they taste, how sweetly they bounce when I'm thrusting inside her—because I can. Fuck the public. Fuck the stockholders. Fuck everyone who's watching our family like we're the latest high-society car crash, snapping photos instead of offering a hand.

This is my woman.

My fiancée. Soon to be my wife.

"Does Mom know?" I ask, rueful as I imagine her reaction.

Hemingway looks faintly mystified, the same way he does when I helped him study chemistry. "She did the same thing as Eva. She laughed." He makes his voice into a falsetto. "*This is what people find scandalous these days? Back in my day, we had real scandals."*

A few years ago she would have sent me an email reprimand for a video like this.

Then again, a few years ago, she wouldn't even have been in the state.

She's changed. I've changed, too.

And Dad? Well, Dad. He's loved, and respected, and even, sometimes, by the general public, feared. What more can a man ask for, if this is really going to be the end?

We take our seats. Mom returns with some Starbucks contraband, since it isn't sold in the hospital. "I also found this," she says, holding up a bottle of Bailey's Irish Cream.

Eva shakes her head no but accepts the latte gratefully.

I only want black coffee. So it's only the underage Hemingway, along with our mother, who have a liberal splash of the sweet, milky liqueur in their paper cups.

Mom downs a double espresso in a single shot. "I needed that."

Hemingway takes a sip and coughs. "What exactly is this?"

I smirk. "Can't handle it?"

"I mean the alcohol is fine. Espresso, though."

"Pansy," I say, not without affection.

"What? I'm just an innocent child, being corrupted into the ways of caffeine."

I snort a laugh. This is… nice. Something I never thought I'd say about sitting in a waiting area outside an operating room, waiting for news of my father's surgery.

Like we're a family.

Because, I suppose, we are again.

Eva did that for us.

The surgery was supposed to last three hours, but it goes for five. That's probably not a good sign, but I need to have faith in the doctors. And in my father. And in the universe, which would be ludicrous if Eva hadn't taught me how to hope again.

Finally the doctor comes out, her dark hair askew from being under the cap for so long, her eyes wild—as if she's just hiked through the wilderness back to civilization. We gather around her, Eva at my side. Hemingway holds hands with Mom.

"I won't lie," Dr. Khan says, "It was a tough surgery. It was a bad break, but we were able to reconstruct it. We had to make larger incisions than I would want, but it was better than having to do a hip replacement. He's in recovery now, and you'll be able to see him soon.

"Thank God," Eva murmurs.

Mom asks about the recovery process, which sounds long and painful.

"The risk for someone at his age with his surgery is high. The next six months will be important. We'll watch closely for any sign of infection as well as depression, which are risk factors. The good news is, though, that he's in strong health."

I open my mouth to object, but the doctor sees it and shakes her head.

"Heart disease, a history of strokes, diabetes. Those are the conditions that would make this situation more severe. The dementia—" She pauses, as if to acknowledge the public referendum on medical privacy that's been happening around his disease. "It probably won't make the recovery worse. In fact there's a chance it will make it easier."

"Who knew?" Hemingway says. "There's actually an upside."

A few hours later we're able to see my father—one at a time.

I find him in a recovery room where a nurse still watches his vitals from a machine and another does something with bandages in the corner. No privacy, but I think I'm done with that. Not because I'm going to streak naked through Wall Street, but because I'm going to stop pretending like hiding problems makes them better.

"Hello," he says without recognition. "Are you a doctor?"

"No." I'm too choked up to say more, especially when I see him alive and alert. I used to want more than that, I used to want him to recognize me. To be himself—the self that I recognized as my father. But now that I've almost lost him, I realize how precious it is to have him. Not only his body, as if it's an empty husk. This other person that I've gotten to know over the past few years. Curious and innocent and... usually kind.

He looks down at my suit, which is now irredeemably rumbled. "You here to collect my payment for all this?" he asks, waving his hand at the machinery he's hooked up to.

I shake my head, unable to speak.

There's a blank, pleasant expression on his face, and I realize what's missing.

Ambition. Determination. That strive for something more.

Or as they'd talk about it on TikTok—hustle.

We're never really happy, are we? Human beings, I mean.

When we have more money, we want more. When we have great sex, we want more. (Case in point: the way I yearn for Eva with every breath.) When we're well rested, we have the urge to be productive so we'll be tired again.

People say that if they only had a million dollars they'd be happy but studies, as well as my experience living among the rich and powerful in New York City, prove that isn't true. Because once we have a million, we start spending it. Then we want even more.

Even a billionaire like Daniel Hughes had felt the drive. The fierce responsibility to his employees and stockholders. The need to train his sons. The requirement of secrecy.

And now, with all of that gone, he's... happier.

Maybe there is an upside. As insane as that sounds to me, maybe there is.

"Then who are you?" he asks.

Your son. Except somehow, that's not even right. When he's not my father, I'm not his son. I'm something else, though. Someone who still loves him. "Your old friend," I say, my voice hoarse. "I'm your friend coming to check on you."

A smile breaks out on his face, as if that explains everything. And I suppose it does. "Well, I'm feeling fine. Don't even have any pain in my hip, even though they said it's broken."

"That's probably the great drugs they have you on," I say, going for humor.

"Then everyone should be on these," he says earnestly. "All the time. I feel great."

I speak with him for another few moments. Then Hemingway goes in. Even Eva wants a moment with him. She laughs and tells me he thought she was a nurse. She got him another pillow, not minding in the least.

Then it's my mother's turn.

She's been quiet this whole time, subdued.

I'd thought she might not even want to go in, but she stands.

"Mom," I say quietly. "He's not—"

He's not himself.

That's what I was going to say. He's not himself, but that's not quite true. He's a new self. He's someone, even if he's not the Daniel Hughes I thought I wanted.

"It's okay," she says, sounding determined and... loving. "I don't need to talk to him. Not really. I just want to sit with him. Until they kick me out, I'll sit with him."

And I watch her go into the recovery room

with her head held high.

Providing comfort to him. Accepting the peace that's available.

My heart squeezes. He may not be the man she married, but he's a man she loves.

Chapter Nineteen

Eva

Something strange happens.

I would have expected news of Daniel Hughes's fall and serious surgery to foment the public panic into new heights. Instead, the video of us in the courtyard of the hospital resurrects the social media campaign that had started with our fake relationship.

#Finneva trends higher than it ever has, not as an example of wealthy people doing wrong, but instead as a testament to love blooming in unlikely places.

"They're just like us," one TikToker says.

Which is mostly true.

We cling to each other in dark moments. We comfort each other using words and touch and even laughter. We love, because in the end it's the only thing worth a damn.

Then again, in some ways we're different.

Like the fact that Finn donated a new wing to the hospital, complete with funding for an even larger serenity garden. People need medical care to survive, but they need solace, too. Rather than stamping it with the Hughes name, he named it after the doctor who operated on him. They break ground on the Khan Building six months after the surgery.

My sister Sophia says she isn't surprised by the reversal of public opinion, but then she's the most social media savvy out of all of us. My mother shakes her head, still not quite understanding the way opinion spreads like wildfire, before magazines can even print it.

We're sitting in the same room where we were when Finn first stole me away.

Then it had been a refuge during the gala for the Society for the Preservation of Orchids.

Now it's a large dressing room as Sophia measures me.

I'm standing on a footstool which serves as a makeshift pedestal, my hands raised so that my sister can move around me with efficient motions.

"Hmm," she says.

I laugh. "That's not what any woman wants

to hear when she's being measured."

"It's not the measurement that's tricky," she says, her voice muffled. "It's trying to guess what the measurement will be. How much do you plan to exercise after the baby is born? Are we talking like a cute postpartum bump or Katie Holmes running a marathon?"

"Let's go with a cute bump. No marathons for me."

"Okay," she says. "That makes it easier."

My mother sighs. "If you got married *before* the baby…"

"We've been over this. I want to get married after. That way we'll have more time to plan it. And the baby will get to attend the wedding."

"People will talk."

"People always talk. About everything. Literally."

Sophia peeks around me. "To be fair, the baby would still get to attend if you get married while you're pregnant. But everything would sound muffled through the amniotic fluid."

My mother shudders. "Must you be vulgar, Sophia?"

I grin. "You had eight children, Mom."

"I've blocked out the memories," she informs me. "Especially the births."

"Well, I'm looking forward to it. Even if I am terrified."

"You'll be great," Sophia murmurs.

"Thanks, Sis." I smile down at her. "Now, are you done measuring or what?"

"In a minute." She looks excited. "Wait, does this mean I get to design a dress for the baby, too? It will be *so cute*. I'll need to research baby clothes."

I'm a little hesitant. It was one thing to ask my sister to make my own wedding dress. I told her she could go as wild and avant-garde as her heart desired, which she of course took as a challenge. But to my surprise she said she was going with white.

That's the only thing traditional about it, she'd warned.

I haven't seen the sketches yet, but we have time.

I'm less sure about her making something for the baby.

"It's a boy," I say, doubtfully. "Do you know how to make suits?"

"Of course I can make suits. But it's not like a baby needs to wear a necktie. Boys wear christening gowns, after all. Wait, is your baby going to be Catholic? Is he going to get baptized? Okay,

I'm going to make a christening gown *and* a wedding suit for him."

"I love that you love him."

She glances at my stomach with affection. "Of course I do. I'm going to be the best aunt in the world. The one who gives him a fake ID and scores drugs for him."

I put my hands around my stomach in a protective stance while my mother gasps.

That only makes Sophia laugh. "You guys are so easy to tease."

The door to the sitting room opens.

A man stands there in a tux that speaks of wealth and a bearing that says his family has had it for generations. Privilege. Power. And enough self-awareness to make it feel like an inside joke that you're part of.

Phineas Hughes looks the same as he did before, handsome and charming as hell.

Blond hair gleams beneath the low lighting.

Hazel eyes twinkle with roguish charm.

"Finn Hughes," my mother exclaims, her cheeks pinkening, her eyes going bright. Doesn't matter how many times she sees him or how obvious his flirtatious compliments are, she still blushes whenever he enters the room.

"Mrs. Morelli," he says with a playful bow,

just like he did at the gala last year.

"I told you to call me Sarah," she says, "especially now that you're family."

"Mrs. Morelli," he says, refusing her with so much grace and respect that she can't be offended. "It's always a pleasure to see you again. I came looking for your daughter."

Excitement rushes through me like champagne, like caffeine.

Because no matter how long we've been together, I blush, too.

He's too handsome for his own good.

"I want Eva," he says, glancing at me. That devilish glint in his eyes promises escape from the prodding of a measuring tape. "We have plans."

"You didn't tell me you had plans," my mother says. "Where are you going?"

I grin, because this is just like before. And yet completely different. Because I know him now, the way a man can know a woman. I sense his desire. "Yes, Finn. Where are we going?"

Hazel eyes accept my challenge. "It's a surprise."

"Indeed," Sarah murmurs, glancing between the two of us.

"They're going to have sex," Sophia tells her mother, who gives her a chiding glance.

"Sophia," she says, reprimanding.

Sophia gently tosses the measuring tape in her box and jots down one last thing in the notebook. "Well, far be it for me to cockblock. Have fun, you crazy kids. Be sure to use protection—oh wait, I guess it's too late for that. Then go bareback for all I care."

"Sophia Morelli!"

"Come on," I tell Finn, grabbing his hand. "Let's go before Mom faints."

He takes my hand and leads me out of the room. Out to the car in front of the Morelli mansion. "How about a bet?" he asks as he hands me inside. "If I can make you come by the time we get to your loft, I win. And if you don't come, then you win."

"What do I win?" I ask, my body already strumming with desire.

He reaches into his pockets. A quarter flips toward me, and I catch it between both hands. "Twenty-five cents? I suppose I could add foam to my Starbucks order tomorrow."

His hand tilts my face up, and then he's kissing me, holding me open for a sensual assault, promising things he'll do with his hands during the drive. "You could, but I'll let you in on a secret… you won't win."

CHAPTER TWENTY

Finn

I STAND BEFORE an audience of hundreds of press members and photographers, Eva standing by my side with her head held high. I feel the gravity of the moment, the weight of all the eyes upon us, and I'm determined to make my mark.

I clear my throat and adjust the microphone, then begin to speak.

"I'm here today to make an announcement," I say, my voice coming out clear and strong, despite the implications of what I'm saying, despite the faint tremble of caution. That caution will probably always be there, but my decision is stronger. "I have early-onset dementia, like my father before me. And like his father before him."

The room is silent, all eyes on me, no shouted

questions.

They're shocked into silence.

Not because I have dementia, of course. Everyone knows it's hereditary. It's been the subject of much discussion, whether or not I'm affected, too. Or when it will happen. The shock is that I'm admitting it with cameras trained on me.

"Those of you with experience with dementia know how painful it can be for the families. That's also true for the larger Hughes Industries family, the stockholders and employees who are impacted by what we do here. Which is why I'm choosing honesty. People have a right to privacy. They have a right to illness and weakness and a thousand other things, but I'm choosing to tell you. Because I want to manage it together. Not hide it in the shadows. Not run from it. Not pretend it isn't happening."

Now there's a burst of questions, reporters shouting.

It's enough to cause a hitch in my breath, but I also feel a swell of rightness in my chest. Eva looks serious, her eyes luminous with love and pride.

"The truth is," I say, letting them quiet down so they can hear me, "any CEO may suffer from dementia. Or depression or anxiety. Or cancer.

Or a thousand other things that may impact their work. I'm not promising it won't affect me. What I'm promising is that I'm going to work hard to set up oversight and checks so that it never negatively impacts Hughes Industries."

I pause and look into the crowd.

Every eye is upon me, and I can feel their anticipation.

"This isn't about curing every disease. This is about living with them. Life isn't over because someone might get early-onset dementia." I reach out, and Eva takes my hand. "Someone I love taught me that. And we're going to get through this… together."

With that, the room erupts. There are shouts of approval and clapping. And more questions, though it's impossible to make them out over the clapping. I can feel the energy of hundreds of journalists and photographers.

It's hard to believe that they're applauding for honesty.

I step back, yielding the floor to Caitlyn Laurie, our chief communications officer, who will field the rest of the questions. I take Eva's hands in mine and look deep into her dark eyes. We've come so far together, and now we're on the brink of something even bigger.

A smile tugs at my lips. "Let's do this. Together."

She nods, her eyes shining with love and admiration, and then I take her into my arms for a fierce embrace. I'm supposed to be the one with power here. The CEO. The heir. The billionaire. But she's the one who makes it possible, as we face an unknown future.

Photographers snap pictures of us, but I don't give a damn.

I turn to them and smile. Eva waves.

We aren't hiding from the light anymore.

✧ ✧ ✧

OF COURSE I can't simply drive away from Hughes Industries after that.

Everyone wants to talk, and I'm going to stay as late as necessary to make sure they have their chance. My assurances, for whatever they're worth. And I'm surprised to find out, they're worth a lot. I'm even more surprised by the number of people who come to me with stories.

Of parents with dementia and grief beyond words.

Of secret treatments for cancer and diabetes, executives who were afraid to share the news for fear that they would get fired. Even if it's not fair,

THREE TO GET READY

sometimes the world isn't fair.

They come to me with hesitant hope, one after the other, a steady stream in my office.

By the end of the day, I'm exhausted.

I come back on Saturday to deal with any stragglers.

I'm even in the office on Sunday, but by now it's almost empty.

Everyone has somehow, though I never expected it, moved on.

What Eva said, about people needing time to grieve is happening. They're remembering who signs their paychecks and why they like it. And they're getting over the secrets. Because no matter that I shared the truth in the press conference, the reality is that they won't be privy to every detail of my life—or any of the executive's lives.

The process is not complete, but it's in progress.

Of course, the harder part is still to come.

I was serious about setting up those checks and balances, setting up some kind of test, perhaps every morning, so that I can affirm to myself that I'm fit to lead. Maybe I'll even do it at home with Eva and call in sick if I don't pass them.

I'm still working out the details with Dr.

Faulk.

It will be an ongoing task, though.

A moving target.

I sigh.

Difficult, sure. But we don't shy away from things because they're hard.

The building is always open on Sundays in case people need to get work done, but it's mostly empty. I waved to a couple people on the way in. The lights are off to save power when no one's in a particular department. A soft, golden light illuminates the area, giving it an almost ethereal atmosphere as though it were in suspense. Waiting, perhaps.

A voice comes: "Hey."

I look up and there's Will Leblanc. Eva's brother-in-law. And the previous owner of Summit, a venture capital company we acquired shortly before the news broke. He's young and ambitious. He reminds me of myself, if I had built something from the ground up.

Hungry.

He looks hungry now, though not particularly angry.

"Leblanc," I say.

"Hughes."

"What are you doing here?"

"I came to talk to you." Without waiting for an invite, he comes into the office and sits down in one of the chairs. He makes a show of acting casual, when this visit is anything but.

"You could've made an appointment with my secretary. And brought your lawyer." Because I know why he's here. To fight to take Summit back. To undo the merger. Which will be an absolute fucking mess. Not the best for either Hughes Industries or Summit.

But his lawyer has probably advised him that we'll give in without a fight to avoid the bad publicity. Even if our legal rights are ironclad.

His lawyer is wrong.

Let them come.

"I could have, but I remember us having this great conversation where you said…" He glances at the ceiling, thinking of the words. *"I'm not trying to screw anyone over. Especially someone who's like family."*

Hell. "I did say that."

"Did you mean it?"

"I didn't lie."

He gives me a look. "Don't fuck around. Did you mean it?"

"Yeah. I meant it."

"Then we can work on similar terms. I don't

try to screw people over, either, especially people who are like family, or who are actually in my family. And, yes, I give my brothers shit all the time, because that's what brothers are for. Especially when they're telling you the things you don't want to hear. Hard truths."

It sounds like he wants to stick around. That's unexpected. "Hard truths. Like what?"

"First off, you look like hell."

I snort. "Thanks."

"You've got bags under your eyes and you're in here alone on a Sunday, sighing like you just figured out that your plan backfired on you."

My eyes narrow. I want Summit to stick around, and in fact would enforce a very legal contract, but I'm not going to take shit from him. "Will."

"Which part of what I said isn't true?"

"You don't have any right to decide if my choices backfired. You have no idea what I was trying to do, you sanctimonious ass."

"And you have no right to forge your dad's signature on any number of contracts and agreements, including when you acquired a company from someone who is like family. You could have run the company on your own. You had the legal standing to do it, but you didn't

THREE TO GET READY

want people to know he wasn't involved."

There was no forging, actually, but I don't bother explaining how it went down. Not if he's going to start off with accusations. "Get out of my office."

"Or else you'll punch me? If that's how you want to have this conversation, then let's go down to the warehouse and get in the ring. The floor's softer. It'll hurt less when I kick your ass."

I stare at him, deliberating. I've seen him fight at the underground boxing ring, so I already know he'd kick my ass. This isn't about a physical fight, though. It's a fight of will. Of determination. I could fire this man for the way he spoke to me—and keep his business, too.

But hell, I appreciate honesty.

And like he said, he's family. I let out a short laugh. Which turns into a longer laugh. He thinks he nailed me. "Oh, fuck. You don't have any proof that—"

"I saw your dad at the retirement party. Even if he did sign the documents himself, he wasn't in any state to be agreeing to the terms on behalf of Hughes Industries. And I know for a fact that you didn't force him to sign anything."

"How?" I shake my head, half-mocking. "How do you know that?"

"Because that's not the kind of man you are."

It's not the kind of man I'd be, if things were up to me. If I could have made the decisions as a real CEO, the way Eva suggested. My father wanted things done that way. He wanted to sign documents where he was out of his head. "What kind of man am I, then?"

"The kind that protects his dad at all costs. And I mean every fucking cost. You were never going to stress him out by forcing a pen into his hand, and you'd be damned if you took anybody else down with you. That's where you went wrong, just so you know."

I don't bother correcting him, because he really doesn't know what it's like to be born into this particular legacy. No one does, but I'm done defending my choices. "Tell me more about running a multibillion-dollar international corporation."

"Fair," he says, conceding the point. "You're the one with the massive company, not me. But we can still trade stories. My mom walked out on my dad when I was two, and up until a week ago, I thought she was dead. Turns out she's not."

That's not what I was expecting to hear.

He tells me more about his upbringing, which included an abusive father who not only hit them but locked them in closets. What the fuck. The

THREE TO GET READY

point, though, is that he understands family. And hard decisions. And loyalty.

And he's choosing this.

That's what it comes down to. He's choosing Hughes Industries.

I sigh. "Are you sure you want to do that for me?"

"It's not for you. It's for the money. I'm just kidding. I want a high-stakes challenge, not a bunch of boring corporate bullshit. And I'm not that interested in watching you get screwed over. You're like family. Speaking of, you should be with yours, not sitting in here worrying yourself to death. I say we call it a day. And Monday morning? We hit them with everything we have. Together. Deal?"

He holds out his hand.

After a long moment, I take it. Because I can accept the help of a man who understands loyalty. I'll even win over Alex Wong to my side. I'll rebuild Hughes Industries, not because it's broken, but because it was still being run under my father's reign. That's what no one understands, really. He *was* running the company, because he taught me to run it exactly how he wanted. But now? Now I'm going to run it as the true CEO, a real leader.

And it's time to get to work.

Chapter Twenty-One

Eva

THERE'S A MOMENT during childbirth when I'm sure that I can't continue.

"No," I gasp, hair stamped to my face with sweat, arms shaking with strain. "I can't. I have to get off this ride, Finn. *I need to get off.*"

"You're doing great," Dr. Hoffman says, gently encouraging.

"Can we have a minute?" Finn asks the doctor. When she's gone he turns back to me, his hazel eyes glow a brilliant green. "Sweetheart. What have I done?"

I can only speak through gritted teeth. "He can't come out. He can't."

Finn puts his face close to mine. "You're beautiful and strong. You can do this, sweetheart. I know you can. I believe in you."

Tears run down my cheeks. "I don't believe in myself."

A handsome half-smile from the man in the darkly lit room. "That's why you keep me around. I see the real you. And you're like a goddess right now."

It's hard to imagine, I'm feeling far from a goddess.

I'm sweaty and tired, my voice hoarse from grunting through the contractions. White walls were supposed to be like a cocoon. Classical music over the speakers was supposed to be soothing. All of it felt immediately like nails on a chalkboard. My birth plan has gone to hell.

Another contraction hits like a tsunami, and I let out a scream.

Dr. Hoffman is back in the room. "It's time. I need you to push."

I'm too tired to push, but I can't seem to help it. The pushing takes over my body, until I feel like I'm going to turn myself inside out. I gasp and pant and strain. It feels impossible, what's happening. Like fitting a watermelon through a wedding ring.

Pain, blinding. A strange sensation. Bursting.

Someone shouting. It's me.

And then the garbled cry of a baby.

Intense relief overtakes my body, a physical sensation so strong it takes my breath away. And then he's in my arms, his face wiped clean, the rest of him still coated in nourishing, bloody liquid. "He's here," I say, laughing in a giddy way. "Oh, Finn. He's beautiful."

He puts his arms around both of us. I look into Finn's eyes and see nothing but joy and love radiating from them. I feel so complete in his embrace. The little one in my arms feels like a miracle.

Finn looks choked up, his eyes red. "My God."

"What's his name?" I ask, because we've been unable to choose.

"Daniel," he says, swallowing hard. "After my father. He would be so happy to know it… and I think maybe he will know."

"Daniel," I say, smoothing my trembling hand over his head.

Finn looks down at us with deep tenderness. Our love has grown even stronger over the course of labor. "And then for our next children, we can use the other names."

"I'm never going through that again," I say, and he laughs softly.

Outside the room, our families are waiting.

The Morellis and the Hughes. They gathered one by one during the delivery—first Leo and his wife Haley. Then Sophia. My parents came next. Then Tiernan. And Lucian. Elaine is staying at home watching the kids.

And now they're waiting for a chance to see this child.

I feel a sense of joy and gratitude for this miracle that he's already so loved.

"Do we have to let them in?" he asks, rueful.

"Only for a few minutes."

Leo peeks his head in. "Hey, sister mine."

"Hey," I say with a gentle smile.

That appears to be all the permission they need. He comes in, the rest of the family swarming in after him. They exclaim over the baby and offer her things—food, drinks, cocaine. That last one was Sophia. I find myself surrounded by love, joy, and excitement.

I feel so blessed to have such perfection in my arms.

The days that follow will be filled with sleepless nights, I know, but also tender moments. And pure, undiluted joy as we celebrate the birth of our baby.

Geneva and Hemingway come in, much more civilized and affable compared to my family.

My mother-in-law coos over the tiny boy. "Daniel?" she asks, her voice trembling when Finn tells her what we named him. "He'll love that. He will."

I remember her telling me how Daniel Hughes was so proud when Finn was born.

And I see the same pride in Finn's eyes.

"Are you going to give my brother hell?" Hemingway asks, peering down at the tiny scrunched up face. "Because I support that wholeheartedly.

The baby's tiny cries fill the room.

Finn gives his brother a look.

"Someone's hungry," I say, "I think. I'm still getting the hang of this."

Finn gently but firmly shepherds everyone back out of the hospital room.

I show the baby how to latch on, using the nurse's instructions. The baby's gentle suckling fills the room. My love for him seems to know no bounds.

Even knowing what the future may hold doesn't scare me.

The challenges we face will bring us closer.

We share an unbreakable bond that will only get stronger. I look forward to countless moments of laughter, hugs, and kisses. With Daniel. And with Finn.

Chapter Twenty-Two

Finn

Eva wants to have the wedding at the Hughes mansion, which originally strikes me as odd, but of course I tell her yes. Now I understand why it was so strange. We've kept the secret for so long that the house has become like a mausoleum. A nursing home with a member of one. It doesn't even feel like my house, really. I never invited over friends. It felt almost strange to bring Eva, so vibrant and full of life, to live here.

The wedding is the perfect turning point for the mansion.

It becomes more than walls keeping in secrets.

It becomes a home.

Already my mother has moved back, officially. She still keeps a separate room from my father, but she spends a lot of time with him. And

Hemingway lives here. I asked Eva if she minded... after all, living with your in-laws isn't something most people enjoy. But she said she loved being around family. And besides, she said, referring to her aunt's busy loft, she was used to a crowded living space. She'd find the mansion too empty otherwise.

She brought her terrariums, naturally.

And a few of the pieces from her loft, including a pink and purple giraffe statue that's as tall as she is and a neon sign of the face of the statue of David blowing bubble gum.

Now the air is thick with anticipation as hundreds of guests gather on the lawn of the estate. Columns are decorated with a wealth of orchids. The carpet had been sprinkled with petals, giving the entire area a feeling of warmth and happiness.

At the center of the gazebo, I nervously await the bride.

I didn't expect the nerves to come. I suppose I'm the cliché of a groom, after all. It's not like I'm getting cold feet. If Eva didn't come out, I'd go in after her.

We're getting married today, come hell or high water.

I want her as my wife. I want to be married. So why the hell am I nervous?

Nervous that she'll change her mind?

Maybe.

Nervous that I won't be the husband she deserves?

Definitely.

Some of that comes from the Hughes curse, but it also comes from loving her. Admiring her. Knowing that she deserves the very best. But I suppose, the fact that I'm worrying about being a good enough husband is a good sign.

I'll figure it out.

She's worth that and much more.

I'm wearing a tux with a gold cummerbund and a single pink orchid in the pocket. Gold and pink are the colors of the wedding, with ribbons and flowers and swaths of fabric turning the lawn into a magical place. There are a sea of faces in front of me, but I'm only waiting for one particular face. I'm surrounded by my family and closest friends, but I need Eva.

The music starts, and the crowd watches as the bridesmaids and groomsmen walk through first. Some of my buddies from my younger, wilder days. Along with Hemingway and Sophia, our best man and maid of honor. Sophia carries Daniel in her arms, who's sleeping through the whole thing. It's past his naptime, and he was getting cranky during the prep. For a moment we thought we'd leave him upstairs where my dad can watch from the window.

Don't worry, Eva had said with a laugh, still wearing a white slip, her hair in hair rollers. *Everyone can wait until he's good and ready for this wedding to start.*

And then the music changes.

Eva appears, her dress made of flowy material that loops her. It seems to defy gravity, like white froth on the tips of ocean waves. It's pure white with gold-tinted sparkles, as if dotted with actual stars. It's voluminous in the skirts but slender at the bodice, ending with two ropes of the delicate white fabric that hold up around her neck. She looks… perfect.

Naturally, she holds a bouquet of pink orchids.

A wave of emotion washes over me.

There's a slight blush on her cheeks as she walks down the aisle.

Bryant Morelli walks by her side as they make the long-ish trek down the white aisle runner that's been placed over the green grass.

Every cell in my body urges me to go to her. Be with her. Hold her. I ignored those impulses when I stood in that meeting months ago, listening to Caitlyn Laurie and Heidi Moreland debate my fate. That had been the wrong call, so I don't listen to it now, either.

Restraint has no place in my life.

Waiting doesn't hold any meaning.

So I stride down the white aisle with its pink orchid petals and meet her at the back, where the seats end. Bryant looks surprised and vaguely annoyed. People murmur and turn in their seats, surprised that I'm breaking protocol.

I hold out a hand. "Let's get married, darling."

Eva's eyes twinkle with joy. She's always liked my spontaneity. "Yes, please."

"Don't give a damn if I look eager," I murmur, escorting her the rest of the way down the aisle. "Because I am. Ready for you to be my wife."

I can see the love in her eyes. "I'm ready, too."

This isn't a moment I dreamed of when I was younger, because I never believed it would happen. And yet now it feels inevitable. How could I have wanted to miss this? I didn't know. I didn't know how pure and cleansing love would feel, removing every ounce of doubt.

As we reach the end of the aisle, our eyes meet. A jolt of electric joy courses through my body. I reach for her hands. She squeezes and her warmth and love envelop me. I bend down to kiss her, softly, gently, another break in protocol since I'm supposed to do it later.

"I'd better get a move on," the officiant says, making everyone laugh. "These two look like they're just about done waiting."

The ceremony is beautiful.

"I now pronounce you man and wife."

The guests let out a collective sigh as I take her in my arms again, this time for a thorough, sensual kiss. And there, surrounded by five hundred of our closest family and friends, I make her my wife. We're finally, truly together.

Then we turn to face everyone. I hold up our entwined hands in a victory cheer, and everyone claps. I look out at the crowd with a wave of gratitude and happiness.

We promised to love each other until the end of time.

And I'm determined to keep that promise, no matter what it takes.

Eva looks up at me and gives me a knowing smile.

She understands how deeply my devotion runs. We're now husband and wife, ready to start the rest of our lives together. As the music begins to play and the crowd cheers, we walk hand in hand, ready to begin the journey of our entire lives.

Chapter Twenty-Three

Daniel Hughes

There's music playing.

Something soft and calming as he stares at the night sky. He can recognize the stars. Denebola and Orion and Ursa Major. A sailor has to know. Does that mean he's a sailor? The music plays softly, like water lapping, lapping, an aqueous tinkle.

Faintly he can see the outline of boats, like charcoal drawn on dark paper.

Shadows.

Two dimensional shapes instead of actual things.

The lawn looks real enough, a pale snake of pathways between dark areas that he somehow knows contain colorful flowers.

A big white rectangle is the top of a tent.

He has the memory that it contains people and laughter and familiar music—but he's not sure when that would have happened.

It's empty now.

A woman comes to stand beside him. Beautiful, with long dark-golden lashes and red lips. A gorgeous woman. He knows her from somewhere, but he can't remember.

It seems impossible that he could have forgotten a face like hers.

She looks at him and smiles. "He did it, Daniel. He got married. Even though he swore that he wouldn't. Thank God they didn't take my advice."

"Who got married?"

"Phineas Galileo Hughes. I wanted to name him Daniel, after you, but I think it's right that he has his own name. He chose his own path."

Daniel. His name is Daniel. He wants to ask why she would name someone after him, but it feels like the wrong question, like it might make her smile go away. Instead, he asks, "How was the wedding?"

"Stunning, but you can see for yourself."

She pulls out a phone with a big screen that lights up when she moves her finger across it. Photographs appear on the screen of a handsome young man with a beautiful, dark-haired bride. There are orchids everywhere, white and pink.

As she moves her finger in graceful strokes, more photos appear…

Groups of smiling people in tuxedos and dresses.

A three-tiered wedding cake with orchid petals.

A baby wearing a tiny suit sleeping in someone's arms.

He studies the pictures, looking for someone he recognizes.

Nothing.

Disappointment sounds like a heavy drum.

"It's okay," she says, patient, as if she understands, but how can she? How can she understand when he doesn't even understand?

Everyone in the photos are wearing beautiful clothes. Expensive clothes. Designer clothes, though he isn't sure how he'd know the difference. The woman standing next to him wears a dress that glitters with pale rose. It makes her blonde hair shine even more somehow.

He looks down. He's wearing pajamas.

Somewhere in the house a baby cries. And then is quickly soothed. It's quiet again, but the quiet feels ominous now. Who is he? Where is he?

Why doesn't he know?

Panic makes his heart beat faster. "Who are you?"

She doesn't seem surprised by the question. She comes to stand in front of him and gently links their hands together.

They fit. That's what he thinks as he looks down at their hands, his weathered, hers manicured with nails painted rose gold. Their hands fit together.

"Someone who loves you," she says. "That's what matters."

He looks at her face, both familiar and unfamiliar.

She's both beloved and a stranger to him.

There's music playing, though. Something sweet, like heartache. "I think I love you, too."

Tears appear in her blue eyes, reflecting back stars. "It's true, after all, Daniel. For a while I forgot, but it's true. Love makes everything better."

Epilogue

Eva, many years later

I'M TRYING NOT to act like it's a big deal.

Even though… it is a big deal.

A wedding anniversary would be important to anyone. And a husband forgetting it would normally be grounds for frustration. This isn't a normal situation, though. Dementia treatments have made it so he almost never has flare-ups, but it's always a possibility. No cure is one hundred percent perfect.

The hurt that I'm feeling is totally irrational. At least that's what I tell myself.

Finn came downstairs wearing a polo shirt and jeans, whistling, talking about going to the park to throw the ball around with Danny. I'm sitting here, holding onto my coffee cup like it's going to shatter if I don't keep it together with my bare hands.

"Finn?" I say, my voice wavery. "It's not a regular day."

He turns to me, moving slow, as if it pains him. "It's not?"

"It's our wedding anniversary."

"Today?"

"Yes."

"How many years?"

My throat feels tight. "Five."

"Hell," he says.

"It's okay," I say. "Don't feel bad. I know you didn't mean anything by it."

In fact, in a way it would be easier to handle if I thought it was just regular forgetfulness. Instead I have to worry whether it's an episode. I'll have to write it down in the notebook and bring it up with Dr. Faulk. One slip isn't a big deal... but a wedding anniversary is big.

He's looking away, and I can't imagine his expression. Worry? Shame?

I stand up and go to him, putting my arms around his lean waist. When he looks down at me his expression is carefully blank—but it's a false blankness. A pretense, when he normally doesn't do that anymore. "I'm not angry," I say. "Not about buying a present or anything like that. I wouldn't even have said anything, but I just want to spend the day with you."

"Well," he says, choosing his words carefully, "I suppose you can come to the park with us. Hang out while we throw around a ball."

The park. Throwing a baseball. Not exactly a romantic dinner, but it sounds like heaven anyway. Spending time with the guys in my life—all four of them.

Besides, I can text Soph on the way and see if she can babysit tonight. OpenTable probably has something available, even at the last minute.

We'll still have that anniversary dinner.

We pile into the car—me, Finn, and Daniel. Danny still has to use a booster seat, which he's not particularly pleased about. And Leo babbles as we put him into the carseat. The trunk is overflowing with baseball gear, bouncy balls, and bubbles for the park.

Except when we pull up I realize there's no need for them.

Because the park has been turned into an entire freaking carnival.

A big pink tent stands at the center with a crowd of people. Behind them I can see multiple large bounce houses, a climbing wall, a stand offering popcorn and funnel cakes and other treats. A huge banner across the top says, *Happy 5th Anniversary!*

"Oh my God," I say, barely able to breathe. "You bastard."

"Mommy said a bad word," Hemingway says, and Daniel shushes him.

"You bastard," I whisper, but it's lost all the heat. There are tears in my eyes.

"I did promise you fun all those years ago," he says, taking my hand across the console. "As if I knew the meaning of the word, but I didn't. I didn't know what it would be like to have you as my wife. As the mother of my children. Happy anniversary, sweetheart."

And then he kisses me.

✦ ✦ ✦

Thank you for reading Finn and Eva's emotional roller coaster of a story! We hope you loved this incredibly powerful billionaire love story. And Skye Warren is offering an exclusive bonus epilogue if you want to see more of the happy couple…

Sign up to get the bonus epilogue now >
www.dangerouspress.com/hughes

Other books about the Morelli family include:
- Lucian and Elaine in HEARTLESS
- Tiernan and Bianca in DANGEROUS TEMPTATION
- Sophia and Damon in CLAIM

The warring Morelli and Constantine families have enough bad blood to fill an ocean, and their brand new stories will be told by your favorite dangerous romance authors. See what books are available now and sign up to get notified about new releases here…
www.dangerouspress.com

New York Times bestselling author Skye Warren has another emotional billionaire romance you'll love… THE PAWN is an enemies-to-lovers, revenge romance with a virgin auction by a billionaire with a dark past.

"Wickedly brilliant, dark and addictive!"

– Jodi Ellen Malpas, #1 New York Times bestselling author

The price of survival…

Gabriel Miller swept into my life like a storm. He tore down my father with cold retribution, leaving him penniless in a hospital bed. I quit my private all-girl's college to take care of the only family I have left.

There's one way to save our house, one thing I have left of value.

My virginity.

A forbidden auction…

Gabriel appears at every turn. He seems to take pleasure in watching me fall. Other times he's the only kindness in a brutal underworld.

Except he's playing a deeper game than I know. Every move brings us together, every secret rips us apart. And when the final piece is played, only one of us can be left standing.

Prologue

THE PARTY SPILLS over with guests, from the ballroom to the front lawn. It's nighttime, but the house is lit up, bright as the sun. All around me diamonds glitter. We've reached that tipping point where everyone is sloshed enough to smile, but not so much they start to slur. There's almost too many people, almost too much alcohol. Almost too much wealth in one room.

It reminds me of Icarus, with his wings of feather and wax. If Icarus had a five-hundred-person guest list for his graduation party. It reminds me of flying too close to the sun.

I snag a flute of champagne from one of the servers, who pretends not to see. The bubbles tickle my nose as I take a detour through the kitchen. Rosita stands at the stove, stirring her world-famous jambalaya in a large cast iron pot. The spices pull me close.

I reach for a spoon. "Is it ready yet?"

She slaps my hand away. "You'll ruin your pretty dress. It'll be ready when it's ready."

We have caterers who make food for all our

events, but since this is my graduation party, Rosita agreed to make my favorite dish. She's going to spoon some onto little puff pastry cups and call it a canape.

I try to pout, but everything is too perfect for that. Only one thing is missing from this picture. I give her a kiss on the cheek. "Thanks, Rosita. Have you seen Daddy?"

"Where he always is, most likely."

That's what I'm afraid of. Then I'm through the swinging door that leads into the private side of the house. I pass Gerty, our event planner, who's muttering about guests who aren't on the invite list.

I head up the familiar oak staircase, breathing in the scent of our house. There's something so comforting about it. I'm going to miss everything when I leave for college.

At the top of the stairs, I hear men's voices.

That isn't unusual. I'm around the corner from Daddy's office. There are always men coming to meet with him. Half the people he works with are downstairs right now. But he promised no work tonight, and I'm going to hold him to it, even if I have to drag him downstairs myself.

"How dare you accuse me of…"

The venom in the words stops me on the landing. That doesn't sound like a regular business meeting. Things might get tense around a contract, but there's plenty of back slapping and football talk before and after.

More heated words hover just below the noise of the party, ominous and indistinguishable. I twist my hands together, about to turn around. I won't bother him after all.

A man rounds the corner, almost colliding into me.

I gasp, taking a step back. There's nothing behind me. *The stairs!* Then two hands grasp my arms, hauling me back onto steady ground. I have only a glimpse of furious golden eyes, almost feline, definitely feral. Then he's sweeping past me down the stairs. I cling to the carved banister, my knees weak.

It's another minute before I can detach myself from the wood railing. My breath still feels shuddery from that near miss, from that man's hands on my bare arms. I find Daddy pacing inside his office. He glances up at me with a strange expression—almost like panic.

"Daddy?"

"There you are, Avery. I'm sorry. I know I said no work—"

"Who was that?"

A cloud crosses over his expression. Only now, in the lamp's eerie glow, do I notice the lines on his face. Deeper than ever. "Don't worry about him. This night is all about you."

Now that I've started noticing his appearance, I can't stop. His hair. All salt now. No more pepper. "You know I don't need all this. This party. Everything. You don't have to work so hard."

The smile that crosses his face is wistful. "What would I do if I wasn't working?"

I shrug, because it doesn't matter. My friend Krista's dad plays golf every single day. Harper's mom is on her fourth husband. Anything but plant himself behind a desk, eyes soft with strain. "You could date or something."

He laughs, looking more like himself. "You're the only girl in my life, sweetie. Now, come on. Let's join the party before they trash the place."

His arm around my shoulders pulls me close, and I curl into his jacket. I breathe in the comforting smell of him—the faint scent of cigar smoke, even though he swears he's quit. I lay my head on his shoulder as we pass the chessboard where we play together.

"I'll miss our games."

He kisses my temple. "Not as much as I'll miss you."

"You could download an app on your phone. We could play online."

"I'm lucky if I can make calls on this damn thing," he says, laughing. His expression darkens when he looks at the screen of his phone, reading the text across a white popup background. "Sweetheart, I have to call someone."

Disappointment burns down my throat. Of course he's a busy man. Most of my friends barely know their dads. I'm lucky he's always made time for me. No matter how crazy things get at his business, he always makes time for our chess games. Every week.

I kiss his cheek, seeing the age spots on leathery skin for the first time.

Downstairs I find Justin by following the sound of his laugh. It's a big, booming laugh that I suspect he's practiced. However it happened, it's infectious. I'm already grinning when I enter the room.

He holds out his hand to me. "The woman of the hour."

I fold into his side, tickled by the champagne in my bloodstream and the relief of being downstairs. Whatever happened in that office was tense. Dark. "I was just checking on Daddy."

"Working," Justin guesses.

"Unfortunately."

"Well, I guess you're stuck with me," Justin says, winking at the couple he was talking to. I recognize them as a famous neurosurgeon and his wife, parents to a man running for the state senate seat.

I make my introductions to them. Of course this party isn't only for my high school graduation. Like all the other parties in Tanglewood society, it's about networking. For my father. For Justin, who has big plans to follow his father's footsteps into politics.

"Salutatorian," Justin's saying. "You should have heard her speech about the way the things we do now are the myths of the future."

The man smiles, somewhat indulgent. "She'll be a great asset to you, son."

I manage to keep a pleasant expression, even though I hope to be more than an asset. I want to be his partner. He knows that, doesn't he? Justin has that public smile, the one that's too bright and too white. The one that doesn't mean anything.

By the time we make our excuses, my cheeks hurt from smiling.

Justin pulls me behind a screen, nuzzling my

neck. "Maybe we can sneak up to your room."

"Oh," I say, a catch in my breath. "I think Daddy will be down soon…"

"He won't find out," he murmurs, his hands sliding over my dress, under it. We're not visible to the party, but anyone could walk back here. My heart pounds. His hands are soft and grasping—and for some reason my mind flashes to the man at the top of the stairs, his firm grip on my arms.

"Justin, I—"

"Come on. You turned eighteen two weeks ago."

And okay, I did use that as an excuse before. Because I didn't feel ready. And it has nothing to do with how old I am or how much I love Justin. Maybe if my mother were still alive, if she could have told me the secrets of being a woman. The internet is a terrifying teacher.

I turn in his arms, pushing him to arms' length. "I love you."

He frowns. "Avery."

"But it wasn't just being seventeen. It's everything. I want… I want to wait."

His eyes narrow, and I'm sure he's going to say no. He's going to storm off. *What if I ruined everything?*

By degrees he seems to relax. "Okay."

"Okay?"

He sighs. "I'm not happy about it, but I'm willing to wait. You're worth waiting for."

My throat feels tight. I know it's a lot to ask for, but he's the best boyfriend I can imagine. And Daddy loves him, which is a huge plus. This fall I'll start school at Smith College, the same private all-girls college where Harper's going. Everything is perfect.

That's how it feels in this moment, like flying.

I have no idea that in less than a year I'll fall from the sky.

Chapter One

WIND WHIPS AROUND my ankles, flapping the bottom of my black trench coat. Beads of moisture form on my eyelashes. In the short walk from the cab to the stoop, my skin has slicked with humidity left by the rain.

Carved vines and ivy leaves decorate the ornate wooden door.

I have some knowledge of antique pieces, but I can't imagine the price tag on this one—especially exposed to the elements and the whims of vandals. I suppose even criminals know enough to leave the Den alone.

Officially the Den is a gentlemen's club, the old-world kind with cigars and private invitations. Unofficially it's a collection of the most powerful men in Tanglewood. Dangerous men. Criminals, even if they wear a suit while breaking the law.

A heavy brass knocker in the shape of a fierce lion warns away any visitors. I'm desperate enough to ignore that warning. My heart thuds in my chest and expands out, pulsing in my fingers, my toes. Blood rushes through my ears, drowning out the whoosh of traffic behind me.

I grasp the thick ring and knock—once, twice.

Part of me fears what will happen to me behind that door. A bigger part of me is afraid the door won't open at all. I can't see any cameras set into the concrete enclave, but they have to be watching. Will they recognize me? I'm not sure it would help if they did. Probably best that they see only a desperate girl, because that's all I am now.

The softest scrape comes from the door. Then it opens.

I'm struck by his eyes, a deep amber color—like expensive brandy and almost translucent. My breath catches in my throat, lips frozen against words like *please* and *help*. Instinctively I know they won't work; this isn't a man given to mercy. The tailored cut of his shirt, its sleeves carelessly rolled up, tells me he'll extract a price. One I can't afford to pay.

There should have been a servant, I thought. A butler. Isn't that what fancy gentlemen's clubs have? Or maybe some kind of a security guard. Even our house had a housekeeper answer the door—at least, before. Before we fell from grace.

Before my world fell apart.

The man makes no move to speak, to invite me in or turn me away. Instead he stares at me with vague curiosity, with a trace of pity, the way one might watch an animal in the zoo. That might be how the whole world looks to these men, who have more money than God, more power than the president.

That might be how I looked at the world, before.

My throat feels tight, as if my body fights this move, even while my mind knows it's the only option. "I need to speak with Damon Scott."

Scott is the most notorious loan shark in the city. He deals with large sums of money, and nothing less will get me through this. We have been introduced, and he left polite society by the time I was old enough to attend events regularly. There were whispers, even then, about the young man with ambition. Back then he had ties to the underworld—and now he's its king.

One thick eyebrow rises. "What do you want with him?"

A sense of familiarity fills the space between us even though I know we haven't met. This man is a stranger, but he looks at me as if he wants to know me. He looks at me as if he already does. There's an intensity to his eyes when they sweep over my face, as firm and as telling as a touch.

"I need…" My heart thuds as I think about all

the things I need—a rewind button. One person in the city who doesn't hate me by name alone. "I need a loan."

He gives me a slow perusal, from the nervous slide of my tongue along my lips to the high neckline of my clothes. I tried to dress professionally—a black cowl-necked sweater and pencil skirt. His strange amber gaze unbuttons my coat, pulls away the expensive cotton, tears off the fabric of my bra and panties. He sees right through me, and I shiver as a ripple of awareness runs over my skin.

I've met a million men in my life. Shaken hands. Smiled. I've never felt as seen through as I do right now. Never felt like someone has turned me inside out, every dark secret exposed to the harsh light. He sees my weaknesses, and from the cruel set of his mouth, he likes them.

His lids lower. "And what do you have for collateral?"

Nothing except my word. That wouldn't be worth anything if he knew my name. I swallow past the lump in my throat. "I don't know."

Nothing.

He takes a step forward, and suddenly I'm crowded against the brick wall beside the door, his large body blocking out the warm light from inside. He feels like a furnace in front of me, the heat of him in sharp contrast to the cold brick at my back. "What's your name, girl?"

The word *girl* is a slap in the face. I force myself not to flinch, but it's hard. Everything about him overwhelms me—his size, his low voice. "I'll tell Mr. Scott my name."

In the shadowed space between us, his smile spreads, white and taunting. The pleasure that lights his strange yellow eyes is almost sensual, as if I caressed him. "You'll have to get past me."

My heart thuds. He likes that I'm challenging him, and God, that's even worse. What if I've already failed? I'm free-falling, tumbling, turning over without a single hope to anchor me. Where will I go if he turns me away? What will happen to my father?

"Let me go," I whisper, but my hope fades fast.

His eyes flash with warning. "Little Avery James, all grown up."

A small gasp resounds in the space between us. He already knows my name. That means he knows who my father is. He knows what he's done. Denials rush to my throat, pleas for understanding. The hard set of his eyes, the broad strength of his shoulders tells me I won't find any mercy here.

I square my shoulders. I'm desperate but not broken. "If you know my name, you know I have friends in high places. Connections. A history in this city. That has to be worth something. That's my collateral."

Those connections might not even take my call, but I have to try something. I don't know if it will be enough for a loan or even to get me through the door. Even so, a faint feeling of family pride rushes over my skin. Even if he turns me away, I'll hold my head high.

Golden eyes study me. Something about the way he said *little Avery James* felt familiar, but I've never seen this man. At least I don't think we've met. Something about the otherworldly glow of those eyes whispers to me, like a melody I've heard before.

On his driver's license it probably says something mundane, like brown. But that word can never encompass the way his eyes seem almost luminous, orbs of amber that hold the secrets of the universe. *Brown* can never describe the deep golden hue of them, the indelible opulence in his fierce gaze.

"Follow me," he says.

Relief courses through me, flooding numb

limbs, waking me up enough that I wonder what I'm doing here. These aren't men, they're animals. They're predators, and I'm prey. Why would I willingly walk inside?

What other choice do I have?

I step over the veined marble threshold.

The man closes the door behind me, shutting out the rain and the traffic, the entire city disappeared in one soft turn of the lock. Without another word he walks down the hall, deeper into the shadows. I hurry to follow him, my chin held high, shoulders back, for all the world as if I were an invited guest. Is this how the gazelle feels when she runs over the plains, a study in grace, poised for her slaughter?

The entire world goes black behind the staircase, only breath, only bodies in the dark. Then he opens another thick wooden door, revealing a dimly lit room of cherrywood and cut crystal, of leather and smoke. Barely I see dark eyes, dark suits. Dark men.

I have the sudden urge to hide behind the man with the golden eyes. He's wide and tall, with hands that could wrap around my waist. He's a giant of a man, rough-hewn and hard as stone.

Except he's not here to protect me. He could

be the most dangerous of all.

A man blows out a breath, smoke curling from his lips. He wears a slate-gray vest and lavender tie. On another man it would have made him soft, but with the two-days' growth on a strong jaw, with the devilish glint in his black eyes he's pure masculine power.

Damon Scott.

"Who do we have here?" he says.

There are other men in the room, other suits, but I don't focus on them.

The man takes a seat near Damon, to the right of him and a little deeper in the shadows, his eyes turned to bronze in the dark. Like he's watching all of us, like he's set apart. I don't focus on him either.

"I'm Avery James," I say, lifting my chin. "And I'm here for a loan."

Damon drops his cigar into a ceramic dish on the side table. He leans forward, pressing his fingers together. "Avery James, as I live and breathe. I never expected you to visit me."

"Desperate times," I say because my predicament isn't a secret.

"Desperate measures," he says slowly, as if tasting the words, treasuring them. "I'm not in the habit of giving money away for nothing, even to beautiful women."

I find myself searching the darkness for golden eyes. For courage? Whatever the reason, strength infuses me like a thick gulp of brandy. "What do you give money away for?"

Damon laughs suddenly, the rich sound filling the room. The other men chuckle along with him. I'm their source of entertainment. My cheeks flame.

The man with golden eyes doesn't crack a smile.

Damon leans forward, obsidian eyes glinting. "In return for even more money, beautiful. Which is why you have a problem. That high school diploma isn't going to count for much, not even from the best private school in the state."

It wouldn't. And who would hire a James when my father has just been convicted of fraud? Part of me still refuses to see the truth. I keep flinching away from it. Every time it hurts. "I'm smart. I'm willing to work. I'll figure out something. I just need time."

Time to keep the creditors at bay, time to pay for my father's medical care. Time to pray, because I don't have any other options.

"Time." He gives me a crooked grin. "And how much is that worth to you?"

My father's life. That's what hangs in the balance. "Everything."

Golden eyes watch me steadily, measuring me. Testing me.

Mr. Scott huffs an amused breath. "Why would I hand you twenty grand that I'm never going to see again, much less interest?"

More than twenty grand. I need fifty. *I need a miracle.* "Please. If you can't help me—"

"I can't," he says flatly.

Golden Eyes reclines, face half in shadow. "That's not quite true."

The whole room stills. Even Damon Scott pauses, as if seriously considering the words. Damon Scott is the richest man in the city, the most powerful. The most dangerous. Who can tell him what to do?

"Who are you?" I say, my voice shaking only a little.

"Does it matter?" Golden Eyes asks, his tone mocking.

Righteous anger mixes with desperation. I'm already in a free fall—why shouldn't I spread my arms? "Who are you?" I say again. "If you're going to decide my fate, I should at least know your name."

He leans forward, the light adding amber to

his lambent gaze. "Gabriel," he says simply.

My heart stops.

Scott smiles, his eyes crinkling with pleasure. He's relishing this, anticipating it. It's almost sexual, the way he watches me. "Gabriel Miller. The man your father stole from."

Gabriel Miller smiles faintly. "The *last* man he stole from."

Oh, and he made sure my father could never steal again.

Never do *anything* again.

Pinpricks against my eyes. No, I can't cry in front of them. I can't fall apart at all, because my father is lying in a bed, unable to get up, hardly able to move—because of what this man did.

This is the man who turned my father in to the authorities.

This is the man who caused my family's fall from grace.

I push down the knot in my throat. "You—" A deep breath, because it's taking all my self-control not to launch myself at him. "You're a murderer."

If Scott is the king of the underworld, Gabriel Miller is a god. His empire extends across the southern states and even overseas. He buys and sells anything worth money—drugs, guns. People.

My father warned me to stay away from him, but then why did he secretly take bribes? Why did he betray Gabriel Miller, knowing how dangerous he was?

My father isn't dead, but without a heavy dose of pain medicine, he wishes he were.

"I've killed men," Gabriel says, standing to full height. I can't help but step back a little. Would he hit me? Worse? His eyes narrow. "When they lie to me. When they steal from me."

Like my father did.

That same sense of falling turns my stomach. I know I should be terrified, and I am—but I've been locked up in a cage my whole life. Part of me enjoys the wind against my face. "I didn't steal from you."

Scott gives a short nod, acknowledging that horrible truth. "His money still paid for your pretty shoes, didn't it? The yoga classes that built that beautiful body?"

And my father paid a terrible price for that money. I still remember him bloodied, broken. Someone sent men to break him. Was it the men that my father double-crossed Gabriel Miller for?

Or was it Gabriel Miller who ordered my father beaten?

I force my shoulders back. "You said you

could help me."

Whatever happens next, I'll face it with honor, with courage. With the same sense of strength I believe my father had. How had he taught me about honesty while lying the whole time? The James name used to mean something, and I'm trying to maintain the last shreds of our dignity.

"Take off the coat," Gabriel says, his tone almost mild.

Everything inside me turns cold, bones frozen, breath a cold blast of air in my lungs. "Why?"

"I want to see what I'm working with. Don't worry, girl. I'm not going to touch you."

With shaking hands I untie my coat and let it slide from my shoulders. There are indistinct murmurs from the men around me—approval, interest. I have the sudden sense that I'm in the center of a bullfight, a stadium full of spectators hungry for blood.

Finally I meet Gabriel's eyes, and what I see is a fire of desire, red and orange and yellow. The blaze scalds me from four feet away. The businesslike clothes I chose to wear don't show much of my skin, but they show all of my shape. The flame of his hunger licks over my breasts, my waist, down my legs.

"Lovely," Damon Scott murmurs. "But a

beautiful body isn't enough. You need to know how to use it."

I shiver. He owns a string of strip clubs all over the city. "I can…learn."

Something flashes in Gabriel's eyes. "You don't know how to please a man, girl?"

There had been stolen kisses, furtive touches in the darkened hallways outside society parties. Justin had pushed me, but I had pushed back. Something had always kept me from letting him have sex with me. And then my family name was disgraced.

You have to understand, Avery. I want to be a senator someday. I can't do that married to a James now.

That was the day after the indictment.

In light of that impersonal phone call, I knew our relationship wasn't about respect. It wasn't about love either. Definitely not pleasure. No, I have no idea how to please a man.

"I'm a virgin," I say softly, sadly, because even if this ruins everything, I can't lie about it. Not when Gabriel Miller has confessed to killing men who lied.

Not when it would be so easy to confirm.

Damon Scott's eyes widen, and something sparks in them, interest where there had been only denial. "A virgin, Avery James? Are you serious?"

A flush turns my cheeks hot. It might seem strange for a nineteen-year-old woman not to have sex, but I went to St. Mary's Preparatory Academy in high school, an all-girl's Catholic school. My father was protective, only allowing me out at night to society events he also attended. By the time I left for college, I was already engaged to Justin.

Gabriel makes a low sound, almost a growl. "She's serious."

Damon Scott looks conflicted. "She's too young."

"You have younger girls dancing at your fucking clubs."

Except they aren't talking about dancing. The thought makes my heart stop. They're talking about selling my body for sex. My virginity. "No," I whisper. "I won't do it."

"You see," Damon Scott says. "She won't do it."

Gabriel's gaze sweeps over my body. He meets my eyes, his expression intent. "She doesn't have a choice. It's the most valuable thing she owns."

It's not a *thing*, I want to scream. This is my body.

Except he's right. It's the most valuable thing

I own—the only thing of any value left after the criminal fines and restitution had been paid, after the lawyers and the bill collectors.

Challenge burns in Gabriel's eyes. He knows how desperate I am. He's the one who made me this way. Does he enjoy seeing me brought low? I wasn't the one who betrayed him, but like Scott said, it was still his money paying for my tuition, my clothes.

"How much?" I ask, the hard knot in my stomach a sign I've already lost.

Damon Scott gives a small smile. "We'll have an auction."

I've been to auctions before—of paintings, antique furniture. The audience with their glasses of wine and numbered signs for bidding. I imagine myself up on the stage. "Who would attend?"

There's a hungry gleam in Damon Scott's eyes. "I know a good many men who'd love to teach you the art of pleasure."

I seriously doubt that I'll feel any pleasure with a strange man, one who prefers to purchase a woman rather than date her. "How long would I have to—"

"A month," Gabriel says, his eyes a bright flame.

Scott is silent a moment. "That would bring in more money."

A month? God, what could a man do to me in a month? Even the thought of being with a stranger for a single night makes my stomach turn over. Bile rises in my throat. Would he want to sleep with me every day? More than that?

"What if—" I swallowed hard. "What if he hurts me?"

Scott shrugged. "It always hurts the first time. So I've heard."

I always imagined that I would have sex with my husband, that he would take care to make it easier for me. A man who paid for the privilege would have no reason to restrain himself. "I mean worse than that. You know…kinky stuff."

"Kinky stuff," Gabriel says, the corner of his mouth turned up. "What do you know about kinky stuff?"

My face feels hot. "I've seen the movie, okay? I know about things."

That's a lie. I squirmed through the movie, lips parted in shock. How did people think of this stuff? Why would any girl like it? And I'm not just a random face in this city. My picture has appeared in the society papers. People know my father. Maybe some of the men were cheated by him, just like Gabriel. Would they want to hurt me in revenge?

"Tell me what you know," Gabriel says.

The words are mocking, but something sparks inside me. "I know that some men like to hurt women. I know it makes them feel big and strong to hurt someone weaker."

"And are you weak, little virgin?"

No, I want to say. Except I've lost everything in the past two months. My life, my school. My friends. I'm a shadow of my former self. *Little virgin* makes me fight back, though. Gabriel makes me fight back. "I'm doing what I have to do. Is that weak?"

His gaze flickers over my body, the yellow of his eyes brighter in the lamp's glow. When he meets my eyes, there's a begrudging respect. "Scott will screen the men who get invited."

"Naturally," Scott says. "I'm not promising these men won't want kinky shit, but they'll respect reasonable boundaries."

That sounds a little vague—what qualifies as reasonable? But I would be stepping into their world, one with thorns and dark shadows. It would be dangerous.

It would be immoral. Daddy taught me to protect myself, but then he failed to protect me. I don't know what to believe anymore. "I don't—I don't know if I can do this."

Scott waves a hand as if it doesn't matter to him. Maybe it doesn't. "Go home, think it over. Come back tomorrow if you want to do it."

I take a step back, relieved to be dismissed. The thought of making a decision hurts my heart, but at least I have a reprieve.

"Oh, and Avery," Scott says thoughtfully. "If you do come back, bring some lingerie. We'll want to get some pictures circulating to generate interest."

I imagine myself undressed down to my bra, my underwear. More exposed than I am now. And photographs would last forever. That would only be the beginning, because when a man purchased my virginity, he could see every part of me. Touch every inch of my skin. Invade every place in my body. My eyes turn hot with tears. All I can manage is a curt nod, and then I'm practically running from the room.

I'm already in the hallway when I feel a hand on my wrist. Something inside me snaps, and I turn back with a cry of anger, of grief. Of defeat. I strike out with an open palm, trying to hit him, *hurt* him.

Gabriel subdues me with another hand on my

wrist.

One step forward and he backs me into the wall. The rich wood paneling is cool through the cloth of my shirt. His body radiates heat at my front. I shrink against the unforgiving wall as if I can get away from him. He closes the space until we're a breath away.

"I was going to say you forgot your coat," he murmurs.

Then I see my trench coat draped over his arm. He's doing something nice, and I just freaked out at him. God, I'm so messed up inside—fear and shame churning in my stomach. "I'm sorry."

"You're right to fight me. I'm not a nice man."

And he was the one to suggest the auction. His hands are still holding my wrists against the wall, and I realize how exposed I am. "Are you going to let me go?"

His lips brush my temple. "Soon, little virgin."

"Don't call me that." My voice trembles only a little, revealing the turmoil inside me.

"What else should I call you? Princess? Darling?"

"You could call me by my name."

He dips his head, his mouth right by my ear, his voice just a breath. "There's only one thing I'm going to call you. *Mine.*"

The possession in his voice makes me shiver. "Never."

But a little voice inside my head says, *Not yet.*

He steps back with a quiet laugh. "You can run away, little virgin. But you'll come back."

I'm very afraid he's right.

Chapter Two

There used to be gardeners working outside and the part-time chef in the kitchen. Maids working under the direction of the housekeeper. Ten thousand square feet of French architectural splendor doesn't tend itself.

When the scandal hit, things got even louder.

The phone rang constantly with Daddy's lawyers and business partners. The long street leading up to the cobblestone driveway became a gauntlet, teeming with reporters. There was even a protest once, with posters that read *Clean Up Corruption* and *Get Out of Tanglewood.*

Once-rounded bushes have grown wild, casting jagged shadows on empty pavement.

No one greets me as I walk through the front door. I follow the faint hum of machinery down the hallway and into my father's bedroom, where a hospital bed has replaced the crackled leather chairs in front of the fireplace.

Rosita looks up from her book with worry. "How was it?"

"Oh, it was fine." I told her I had a meeting

with some businesspeople.

She doesn't know the specifics, but she knows we're desperate for money. The empty rooms where oriental rugs and antique furniture used to sit are proof enough. I've sold everything, scraping every last penny from my late mother's loving decorating. Only my father's bedroom remains untouched—except for the IV drip and health monitors that help keep him alive.

I touch my father's hand, the skin papery. "Did he wake up?"

She glances at my father's resting face, her expression sad. "He had a few minutes of awareness soon after you left, but the drugs put him to sleep again."

Sadness is better than wariness, and definitely better than hatred, the way most of his former staff looked at him during those dark days. He had given them each a small severance package, which was nullified by the court once reparations were ordered. Millions of dollars of reparations depleted every one of his accounts.

And then he'd been attacked, beaten nearly to death.

I know on some level he deserved those things. The censure, the debt. Maybe even the beating, by some morality standards. But it's hard to believe that when I see him struggling to breathe.

I dig through my purse for the bills tucked inside.

Rosita puts her hand over mine. "No, Miss Avery. It's not necessary."

It's easier to force a smile now that I've had practice. "It *is* necessary. And it's fine. Don't worry about me."

She shakes her head, dark eyes mournful. "I'm not blind." A pointed glance at my body. "I see how skinny you've gotten."

I cast a worried look at my father, but he's still asleep. "Please."

"No, I can't take your money." She hesitates. "But I can't watch your father either."

I open my mouth, but my pleas catch in my throat. How can I ask her to come back? She's the only one of our former staff to come at all. And she's right that I don't have the money to keep paying her. It's not her fault I'm running out of options.

"Okay," I say, my voice breaking.

"Your mother—" She makes a soft sound. "She would have been heartbroken to see this."

I know that, and it's the only solace I have in her death. She never had to see my father's fall from grace. She never had to see her little girl turned into a whore. "I miss her."

Rosita's gaze darts to my father, almost furtive. "She was loyal," she whispers. "Like you."

I nod because it isn't a secret. Everyone knew she was a doting wife and mother. A true society maven, friends with everybody and the picture of grace. I always dreamed of being like her one day, but I know that with the visit I made earlier, my life will be irrevocably changed.

"Be careful," Rosita finally adds with a pat to my hand. She takes one final glance at my father. "Mr. Moore is waiting in the back parlor."

My heart thuds.

Uncle Landon has been my father's friend and financial advisor for years. They played golf and the stock market. But even as close as he was, he never would have been invited to the back parlor. That was only for family, which is why the lumpy, comfortable couch wasn't worth anything.

I paste on an expression of nonchalance. "I'll speak to him when I'm done here."

Without another word, Rosita shows herself out. Steady beeps fill the space she left behind, clinical reminders of my father's tenuous hold on life.

Swallowing hard, I take his hand. This hand

rocked me to sleep and tossed a softball. Now it seems cold and frail. I can feel every vein beneath the paper skin.

Tears rise up, but I fight them back. "Oh, Daddy."

I really need my biggest supporter right now. I need someone to tell me everything will be all right. There's no one left to do that. The only thing that will help now is a phone call from one of the city's crime lords. A rich man with money enough to buy a woman for the night.

His eyelids are shot through with blue-green veins. They open slowly, revealing the flat gaze he's had ever since the conviction. "Avery?"

"I'm here. Do you need anything? Are you hungry?"

He closes his eyes again. "I'm tired."

He's asleep most of the time. "I know, Daddy."

"You're a good girl," he says faintly, his eyelids fluttering.

My throat feels thick. "Thank you," I whisper.

"My little jumping jack."

His voice fades to nothing by the end, but I know what he said. He used to call me that when I was little, boundless as little girls can be. He taught me chess to help me focus. And then he found time to play a game with me every week, no matter what. He worked nights and weekends, but he always made time to sit across the chessboard from me.

In the beeping quiet that follows, I know he's asleep again. I only get a few minutes with him a day. The rest of the time the medicine keeps him under, but without it he's in intense pain. He has always been a man of vitality, of action. Multiple broken bones and a harrowing night in the dark alley where they left him aged him twenty years. This is all he has left—the security of this room and the pain medicine. I can't take those away.

"Everything will be okay," I say out loud because I have to believe that. I have to believe that I'm doing this for a reason. Have to believe that it will be enough.

There's no one left to save us except me.

Thank you for reading this sneak peek into THE PAWN! If you want to read more of Gabriel and Avery, be sure to one-click their story on Amazon, Barnes & Noble, Apple, and other book retailers.

About Midnight Dynasty

The warring Morelli and Constantine families have enough bad blood to fill an ocean, and their brand new stories will be told by your favorite dangerous romance authors.

Meet the oldest Morelli brother in his own star-crossed story...

I've known all my life that the Constantines deserved to be wiped from the face of the earth, only a smoking crater left where their mansion once stood. That's my plan until I see her, the woman in gold with the sinful curves and the blonde curls.

In a single moment, she becomes my obsession...

Elaine Constantine will be mine. And her destruction is only my beginning.

My will to dominate her runs as deep as the

hate I have for her last name. No matter how beautifully she bends beneath my hands, I'll leave her shattered, a broken toy for her cruel family.

Winston Constantine is the head of the Constantine family. He's used to people bowing to his will. Money can buy anything. And anyone. Including Ash Elliot, his new maid.

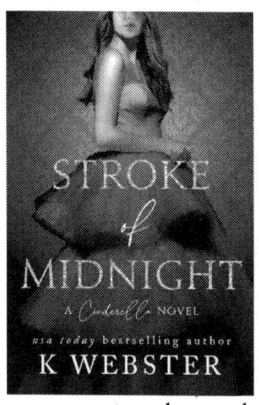

But love can have deadly consequences when it comes from a Constantine. At the stroke of midnight, that choice may be lost for both of them.

"Brilliant storytelling packed with a powerful emotional punch, it's been years since I've been so invested in a book. Erotic romance at its finest!"

– #1 New York Times bestselling author Rachel Van Dyken

"Stroke of Midnight is by far the hottest book I've read in a very long time! Winston Constantine is a dirty talking alpha who makes no apologies for going after what he wants."

– USA Today bestselling author
Jenika Snow

Ready for more bad boys, more drama, and more heat? The Constantines have a resident fixer. The man they call when they need someone persuaded in a violent fashion. Ronan was danger and beauty, murder and mercy.

Outside a glittering party, I saw a man in the dark. I didn't know then that he was an assassin. A hit man. A mercenary. Ronan radiated danger and beauty. Mercy and mystery.

I wanted him, but I was already promised to another man. Ronan might be the one who murdered him. But two warring families want my blood. I don't know where to turn.

In a mad world of luxury and secrets, he's the only one I can trust.

"M. O'Keefe brings her A-game in this sexy, complicated romance where you're left questioning if everything you thought was true while dying to get your hands on the next book!"

– New York Times bestselling author K. Bromberg

SIGN UP FOR THE NEWSLETTER
www.dangerouspress.com

JOIN THE FACEBOOK GROUP HERE
www.dangerouspress.com/facebook

FOLLOW US ON INSTAGRAM
www.instagram.com/dangerouspress

About Skye Warren

Skye Warren is the New York Times bestselling author of dangerous romance with over two million copies sold. Her books have been featured in Jezebel, Buzzfeed, USA Today Happily Ever After, Glamour, and Elle Magazine. She makes her home in Texas with her loving family and wild pack of dogs.

Sign up for Skye's newsletter:
www.skyewarren.com/newsletter

Like Skye Warren on Facebook:
facebook.com/skyewarren

Join Skye Warren's Dark Room reader group:
skyewarren.com/darkroom

Follow Skye Warren on Instagram:
instagram.com/skyewarrenbooks

Visit Skye's website for her current booklist:
www.skyewarren.com